I am BROKE....! LOVE Me

when love and recession struck.

I am BROKE....! LOVE Me

when love and recession struck.

Animesh Verma

Srishti
PUBLISHERS & DISTRIBUTORS

Srishti Publishers & Distributors
N-16, C. R. Park
New Delhi 110 019
srishtipublishers@gmail.com

First published by Srishti Publishers & Distributors in 2010

5th impression

Typeset in AGaramond 11pt. by Suresh Kumar Sharma at Srishti

Printed and bound in India

Dedicated to the youth of my nation.....

ACKNOWLEDGEMENT

First of all I would like to express my deepest gratitude and sincere thanks to my parents without whom I would not have existed. Thanks Dad (Vijay Kumar) for your constant support, motivation and encouragement. You are simply the BEST. Mom (Alka Verma), it's because of your constant blessings that I am able to exist and write. You always gave me full liberty to do whatever I wanted to do in my life and always encouraged me in doing anything I wanted to do. Thanks for everything.

Life is incomplete without friends and this beautiful relationship touches everyone. I would like to express my deepest gratitude to all my friends who always boosted my confidence to write. Varun helped me a lot even did the proof reading of my book; took time out from his busy professional life and shared many new ideas. Dude, you have proved that friends can be banked upon anytime but I can't say thanks to you; I will definitely not say thanks to you coz I love troubling you and I know such words of appreciation hardly fit in with our friendship. We know we are there for each other. I would like to express my deepest gratitude to Abhinandan, my school friend who always motivated me to write more; Gajendra, Chandan, Rishikesh, Balwant, Pranaw, Abhisek Rathore, Bankim, Rajeev and Vinod for their valuable suggestions and inspiring words. I would like to say thanks to all my ex class mates in IIT, Hindu College, D.U. It's because of your good wishes I am able to write. I would like to say thanks to Soumya, my junior in Hindu College who has shared her small poem in my book. I fully appreciate your effort.

Life started from school continued in college till we became professionals. I would like to express my deepest gratitude to my school, Beldih Church School (Jamshedpur); Hindu College and IIT Bombay which inculcated in me the confidence to move on in life. All three academia rock and provide the best education one could get in life. I would like to thank all the teachers and professors who moulded my career. I express my deepest gratitude to Dr. Krishna P. Kaliappan, Dr. Anju Srivastava for their motivating and inspiring words. You were simply the best teachers one could get in their entire life.

Lastly I would like to express my deepest gratitude to Abhisek Verma and Abhisek Rathore who helped me a lot in plotting this script. Your ideas and suggestions were precious to me.

I started writing this book while I was in my last semester of Indian institute of Technology, Bombay. I am always influenced by section of the society called YOUTH or the so called Y generation. I would like to dedicate my book to the youth of the country... You all were my source of inspiration......

An anonymous mail

A high paying job, a superhot girlfriend, a luxurious life, envious friends, and a carefree attitude; this was my life. 'Living life king size'

MONEY...the most important ingredient of life; the one who has it is ecstatic; the one who doesn't have it is a loser and curses him. Who said Money is not everything? Money is the force that gives you all the luxury in life. Money buys many relationships if not all; girls go gaga over it, just observe the world the most beautiful lady in the town, in your college or in your locality, they will be with a guy who at least has a big car or a super cool racing bike, they dine in big restaurant, go to discotheque and enjoy.

I was one such youth, hardly believed in true love; slept with many but loved only one. An investment banking job was a big deal in my life, all my dreams were about to be achieved or rather shattered. I was dining in the most expensive restaurants, playing roulette in the biggest gambling zone of America, was having the company of hot ladies, drinking Black label whisky, smoking expensive cigarettes and travelling around the globe in business class Boeing flight. My luck had taken a U turn just few days back when I was catapulted to overnight success after I bagged the sought after finance job. I was busy enjoying my life; I was carefree.

But soon in the harsh terrain of economic turbulence, company started to lay off employees. There was a panic in the entire finance sector. Money comes with happiness and departs by snatching everything from life. Lots of relationship was broken, many lost their girl friends coz girls do not want to stay with losers. Many lost the hope of living and killed their family, many lost their temper after losing money on the stock exchange but still some relations survived in the turbulent weather and these were the relations which were genuine and lifelong. Many kept on searching for new jobs and then I had my own story.

I saw the recession at a very early age of my career, followed by some incidents that happened in India which made me think like a youth as a force or rather a young gun of India than a mango man (*aam junta*). I lost to my fate just to find myself.

I was broke financially and broken from heart. My love, my friends, my job and my luck all had departed from me; I was in search of them. But I never thought that an innocent and a carefree guy like me could ever hold a pistol loaded with bullets to kill humanity. She was the most beautiful girl I had ever seen in my life, I had some lifelong friends and then everything was destroyed.

I was just another carefree youth like you; the atrocious circumstances have changed me. Now I am a different person trying to fight against the law and order. I would like to bring in front of you a small original story of mine; name it whatever you want, sell it where ever you want but do write this as this feeling of youth should be spread to the entire nation.

Regards,

Armaan

I always wanted to write on youth; I downloaded the file. And then I started reading it.......

When Recession Struck...

Dear Armaan,

I hope you are enjoying your overseas job. You have performed your job with excellence and this was the reason why you were promoted so early in your career and were called here to the headquarters of the bank in the U.S. But due to the ongoing financial turbulence and meltdown, the management has decided to shift you back to our Indian office because we want to reduce overheads here. You will be called back to the U.S office when things get under control. We are really sorry for the inconvenience caused but as a responsible employees of this organization we too have to take some important decisions to make sure that we still remain the best in the market. I hope you would cooperate with us in such a turbulent time. You can join our Indian office from tomorrow; your air ticket is on your desk. I hope you will add same value to the bank there and would work with the same efficiency. We will call you back as soon as the situation calms down.

Happy Journey.

Regards,

M. Smith,

CTO,

Money Bank.

I saw the mail lying in my inbox; I couldn't understand why a fucking fresher has been transferred who is paid so little as compared to others. I always knew my bad luck would never leave me and haunt me wherever I would go. I found the air ticket kept on my table; a letter was also enclosed with it. It was my new salary statement which was reduced drastically as compared to my present salary. I took my letters and belongings from there and attended a small valedictory function from my American colleagues. The American colleagues were quite decent as compared to my Indian colleagues; at least the Americans had the courtesy of never making me feel that they were envious of my overnight success. The American colleagues presented me a Swiss watch; probably they wanted me to realize the hard time which was hovering around the finance sector. Even the colleagues who were envious of me because of my overnight success came to bid me farewell.

The American beauty Miss Maria who was the member of our group came in her hot dress and offered to dance with me. Miss Maria had a perfect figure; white complexion with a tint of pink in it and she always dressed like a model on a ramp. Even Mr. Smith, well in his late fifties eyed her. She was indeed the sexiest employee in the bank whom every other employee wanted to date. But she never gave even a look to them; she was always seen with the CTOs, CEOs and M.Ds. Probably this was the reason why she was catapulted to the post of H.R Manager in such a short span of time. Beautiful women are always considered an asset in any company and create a mixture of culture and sex in the company. I didn't know whether it was my luckiest day to dance with the beauty of the West or my unluckiest day to get thrown out of the job.

Anyways; past was over, future got disillusioned. I thought present to be a gift and so emotionally, I held her hand gracefully and danced with her. The other employees charged with testosterone gaped at us. I knew that I would never be called again to the U.S.

I recalled the day when Mr. Smith, the CTO had announced my name as the employee of the month and I was so happy.

Even the hot cleavage of Maria; the most coveted and the attractive part of her body seemed unattractive; the only thing for which I was mad for and always wanted to direct her to my bed.

Finally with a disconsolate soul, I had to say the hard words,' GOOD BYE'

After the farewell I felt quite dejected and felt as if my dreams were shattered and moved to my room. I packed all my belongings and decided to move to THE TIMES SQUARE for one last time. I took my beer and a burger; I was getting nostalgic at the same time.

I sat on a bench in front of the lighted skyscrapers. I wanted to take a nap and dozed off.

The tall sky scrapers, the lighted towers and the busy roads all seemed deserted to me; the illuminated path looked as dark as my career. Finally I took a few reluctant steps to board my flight; I never wanted to leave United States as I knew this was the place where I could have earned a hell lot of money and fame too. I took my seat in the plane; the hot American air hostess brought some beer. I overshot my capacity of drinking and with my head spinning eventually as expected, I dozed off. I went back to the earlier days of my life when I had joined the MONEY BANK in India three months back, I still remembered the day when I was selected from the campus to enter this glittering world of finance. I worked effectively and eventually was promoted to the head quarters in just three months which everyone in the bank was envious of. The thought that I was returning to the same place was lurking in my mind. I had left that place with high pride and a pompous show off too.

The flight reached its destination, and I went out to find my city, MUMBAI as claustrophobic as ever. I had a premonition of the sucking atmosphere of India after having a high time in the city of skyscrapers. I took a prepaid taxi and decided to take some rest before joining the same boring office. I missed my country very much in the U.S, the culture, the crowd, people hanging from trains and buses, the busy streets, the different festivals and above all, the great Indian food. My respect for my great country had increased; one thing which changed in me after going to the West. I never showed to my friends and family that I missed India, I only showed them the money in the West and hid my boredom; showed the glittering world of high paying jobs which was no more than a highly paid clerky job.

Suddenly my phone rang; it was a call from Mr. Malpani, our shrewd boss at the Indian office. I expected a welcome call but never expected my welcome call to be so unwelcoming.

'ONCE IN A CENTURY CRISIS', the voice on the phone shouted at me.

I courteously asked my team leader about the issue.

'This is absolutely stunning. Wall Street has seen very few days like this. Just check out the news…' my boss's voice attenuated as my Sony Ericsson walkman phone's battery ran out.

I reached my hotel; turned on the English news channel to know what exactly had happened as the Hindi 24*7 news expertise in chicken egg story.

'Stock Exchange has rolled down, the shares market is not performing well', said a news channel. I felt as if I had wakened up on a black day on 16th September.

'Oh, fuck...Its 11 am', I rushed to take a bath as I was getting late for my office; after all it was not a public sector bank, so punctuality had to be maintained. I still remember the day when my half day salary was axed due to my casual approach to the job after I reached late in the office but my friends in the public sector bank enjoyed their life.

'I will be screwed today, this is my first day in my Indian office and I am late by 2 hours', I thought as my taxi raced through the western highway.

I hurriedly reached my office to find a long queue of media covering the office.

'It seems that they are here to welcome you', said the taxi driver sarcastically, blinking his eyes.

'Yeah, I know I am an asset to them', I winked at the driver as I paid him the money, exchanged a smile with him and entered my office.

The media continuously kept on clicking the photo of each and every person coming in and going out of the bank.

'What happened, where are the rest of the people?' I asked the gate keeper.

'All have left', he said.

'But where?' I asked him with eagerness and full of prayer that he might say all was well and no bad news anymore.

'Just see the news you will get to know what happened exactly', he said and moved out.

I went inside the bank; the bank had seen no changes in the past three months. The furniture, computer, television everything was the same, unlike the U.S that gives the best infrastructure to its employees. Even the water cooler which we always complained about was in the same dilapidated condition and had pounds of dust in it.

'They just employ us and make us work like a labour for a salary which appears gold to us but for them it is a silly amount. In fact an American would never work at such a low salary. These MNCs know that Indian employees are always ready to work at such prices considering India as a developing nation. This was the harsh fact of MNCs which I came to know while working with them in the West.' I thought, as I moved to catch a glimpse of the news.

The news reader on the channel broke the news which shattered my dreams,' Global stock markets plunged on Monday as the dramatic collapse of US investment bank Money Bank sparked off steep losses across the financial sector'.

'The collapse of the bank has sent a major jolt through global financial markets as it is by far the biggest victim of the credit crisis that started in August 2007 and had been considered too big to fail', said Global Insight economist Howard Archer.

'FUCK', my bag dropped from my hand as the news channel declared the insolvency of the prestigious bank of the world. It was devastating news for a fresher like me who had just joined the glittering job in finance sector.

CNN telecast the entire news from the U.S, the tall and beautiful building of Money Bank had turned into a media center, and almost all the news channels present there were giving their exclusive reports about thousands of employees thrown out of their jobs.

I saw Mr. Steve on the news channel, carrying something in his hand. He had packed his belongings from his office and was moving out but was soon interrupted by a few media persons whom he avoided with all courtesy. Everything seemed as real as I had seen everything in full bloom yesterday.

I reported to my team leader, Mr. Malpani whom I saw checking out of the office. He had a big cartoon in his hand. Probably he had also packed everything from his office room and was about to leave.

'Sir, what happened?' I asked him.

'Sir', he managed a smile in a tough situation like this.

'My Child Armaan. I am no more your Sir. Our bank has declared bankruptcy and we will be thrown out of this job in the next few hours. So I am just packing all my things. You also do it and try for a new job', Mr. Malpani said and left.

"GOOD LUCK for future," he added too.

I thought he meant the F word rather than the L word.

The whole scene was climactic to me; I was filled in with melancholy. I reached a room in the big office which used to be my room when I was working here. They had shut it down and had put a big lock on it, somehow I managed a key from the gate keeper and I started packing my stuff which I had left there while moving to the West. My eyes moistened, voice became low. I felt like a big loser.

'I wish I had chosen some other job', I cursed myself as I packed my stuff.

For the last time I checked my mail box, it had one mail from the M.D of the bank, "We are extremely sorry to announce that we are not able to protect our bank from bankruptcy. And the bank fears closure. So the choice is with you, write a resignation letter or a termination letter will be sent to you in an hour.'

I moved the message to the trash and didn't even bother to reply to my boss.

'Anyways I will be thrown out of my job' I decided not to reply to him. I wondered how the internet was still in use in the bank.

I packed all my stuff and went out of the office. The media people kept on clicking our photos and presented the news about the financial debacle. Suddenly every news channel wanted to have a glimpse of us and they tried to interview each and every employee about this great debacle. They hardly came to our office when the market was in boom but now they think that their TRP will go high by showing losers like us. Suddenly the losers like us became media's favorite heroes.

I reached my room, kept my belongings in a corner. I lighted my cigarette and took a beer from the fridge. I reminisced about the old days of my life when I cracked this job of analyst from IIT Bombay. I had a heavenly drink that day, gave a huge treat to all my batch mates and my friends, only to face such a bad situation. The bill was close to my Dad's salary but who cared! I knew my pockets will be full of dollars after few months.

I opened the door to enter the gloomy room of the hotel, when suddenly someone pushed me hard and yelled at me. I almost fell due to the impetus applied on me and turned back to see who the person was, only to find the room empty and that it was one of my deadliest hallucinations. Suddenly I was reminded of my past and Varun.

I splashed water on my face, the stream of water trickled down my throat as I tried to gulp down all the events that had happened with me. As the water drops passed my throat, I felt an urge to shout at my losses. I again splashed some water on my face and tried to abate my frustration by shouting loudly, my eyes moistened and I sat down infront of the mirror. I looked at the mirror to find a face haunting me, and I wished I could have talked to her. The image in the mirror gave a beautiful smile and disappeared. I was seeing illusions from my past, a past full of events.

I took my belongings and checked out of the hotel. Suddenly I was engulfed by my past as if enquiring of me if I were the culprit.

I took a taxi and decided to move to IIT Bombay where Rajeev, one of my friends resided.

'Hello, Rajeev. How are you?' I called my friend in IIT as I wanted to *chillax* after the unexpected was over.

'I am fine. How are you doing? I saw the news today, it's such a difficult time', Rajeev said.

'And I have been thrown out too like many others. I am coming there and will stay with you as I want something to cherish', I said and did hide the economic reasons behind my action.

'You are always welcome to my room, I will order your favorite kababs', Rajeev said, just to make me feel a bit lighter. Food helps a lot at the time of distress. To me, after New York, kababs were the most coveted thing.

I hang off, the taxi stopped at the red light crossing when suddenly I saw a bike speeding on the road. The couple was in an intimate position on the bike; the girl held the boy tightly.

I was reminded of Dhoom 2's imitation I once carried out with my sweetest darling.

'Vids!!!!!!!!' I exclaimed as I saw the girl's back and came out to see the biker.

'Vidisha, is that you?' a question suddenly popped up in my mind as the biker stopped beside me. I came out of the taxi and went near them to find that she was some other girl. I said sorry to them and moved ahead to my taxi. It was the time when nothing was going my way; even gold would turn into a useless metal by my touch.

'I am so sorry, I thought you were someone else', I said to the girl and proceeded towards IIT.

I didn't know what had happened to me; suddenly my past was in front of me as if it was making me run in a fashion that bolts and green could be shocked up.

I reached hostel 6 in IIT Bombay; one of the palaces where King Armaan once resided.

'Hello Armaan', Rajeev said to me.

I exchanged a smile with my junior friend but the thought of the job loss lurked at the back of my mind and I felt a bit shameful as I had departed from the Institution with a grand, pompous show off.

But probably Rajeev sensed that I was feeling uncomfortable.

'Time is really tough. The financial recession has added greater pain to students like us. We also are not sure about our future and whether we will get a job or not', Rajeev said; which made me feel a bit comfortable.

Rajeev was one of my closest friends and we shared almost everything between us. I started reading some tabloid and news paper, the center of attraction of all the media was the financial collapse. And questions were raised whether it would affect India or not? I was getting tired of reading such news because I had already witnessed it.

I turned the page to find my picture in one of the articles. I always wanted to be in the limelight and wanted my snaps to appear in leading newspapers but I had never thought in my wildest of dreams that I would be there one day because of a failure.

'Hey buddy, I have something special for you', Rajeev said as he unwrapped the kababs of Sunny Bar from the aluminum foil packet.

'It's my favorite kabab. You still remember my taste', I said to Rajeev.

Rajeev smiled,' "Just as a failed candidate cannot forget the subject in which he has failed until he has failed in many, just as a horse cannot forget his grass and just as a tube light cannot forget the electric current which runs it, in the same way how I can forget you and your taste my friend?"

I was really awed by the similes and metaphors used by him.

Rajeev had a very good sense of humor but somehow he always complicated it. But still I was happy to find such a good friend and to have him at such a tough time was a great feeling.

'I have two more surprises for you' Rajeev told me.

I looked suspiciously and asked him, 'What?'

He opened his bag and took out my favorite Romanov Vodka bottle.

I was now more than happy as I wanted to gulp down the entire bottle.

'Oh, yeah. I still enjoy this drink', I said laughingly.

'How did you bring this inside the campus? I guess drinking was prohibited inside the campus and you remember we were fined coz of this thing only', I posed some questions to Rajeev.

'Laws are meant to be broken, I somehow managed to bring it inside by hiding it in my bag' Rajeev exchanged a cunning smile, feeling like Yuvraj Singh after bludgeoning Broad for six sixes in the over.

I had a bath and took a small stroll in the lawn and went to the room.

Rajeev was already busy making the best peg; adding calculated volume of Vodka in a calculated volume of water.

'Anyways, let's drink' I said as he opened the bottle.

In no time we had drunk three quarters of the bottle and reached the inebriated state.

'Let's go to the terrace' Rajeev said in the style of Sholay's Viru.

I accompanied him to the terrace where students were prohibited form going.

'Nothing has changed in the last six months' I said to Rajeev looking at the sky scrapers of Hiranandani Mansion.

'Absolutely nothing, only thing which keeps on changing are the students', he said in a philosophical tone.

'Rightly said' I nodded my head in appreciation of the words spoken by Rajeev.

'So, when did you come here?' he asked me.

'I came here today only to find myself thrown out of this job. They used to call me an ASSET when I was working with them in the U.S. I think they knew that the bank will close down and that is why they sent me away courteously. I went to my office to see a big lock on my cabin, the vodka effect started to control me as I kept on blaming my unfortunate luck.

'I know it's really difficult to digest the situation when one is thrown out, I can't experience your pain as I am just a spectator.' Rajeev said quietly.

The world came crashing down on me and I didn't even get time to shed some tears. I was not able to believe how quickly things had changed and it seemed like I was on a boat which was far from the shore as well as stuck up amidst the stream.

Suddenly we heard some noise near the staircase; we got scared as we thought that the warden was around for a surprise check in the hostel. We hurriedly hid the bottles behind us and pretended to be normal.

Finally a person came in from the staircase, the heavy shadow falling on us made us a little scared and apprehensive about the identity of the person. We couldn't make out the face of the person as it was too dark.

Finally the anonymous person said,' Do you have SUTTA (cigarette)?'

Laughter broke out between us as we recognized the person to be Ankur; another comic character of the hostel.

Ankur was innocuously iniquitous; who never got irritated with anyone and always played pranks and made everyone laugh, a perfectly harmless creature.

'Here comes the fool, see I taught him the art and science of smoking cigarettes (SUTTA) and now he always comes to my room to ask for one Rajeev said in a majestic tone.

Ankur gave a cunning smile and said, 'Take out another cigarette'.

Finally I took out one and gave it to him to quench his thirst.

'So, how are you Sir?' he asked me looking greedily at the bottle of Vodka.

'I am fine, just came today. Why don't you join us?' I said as I knew he wanted to have a peg as his roving eyes were fixed on the seducing Shilpa Shetty on the cover of Romanov's bottle.

'Why not?' he said and gulped down few pegs like water.

'You are a GOD; you cracked a finance job in IIT. You had the most beautiful girl in IIT as your girl friend, you played cricket with excellence. Now you will be a big manager of a finance company', Ankur said using the lingo of IIT in complete ignorance about the situation.

We always doubted Ankur's general awareness I.Q. But he proved today that he didn't have awareness at all and he never read the news paper except for page 3 news which he used to share with us all the time, news of link ups of different Hollywood and Bollywood stars etc. At least this was something on which he had a great command.

I was about to answer him when he asked for another cigarette.

Ankur gave a cunning smile and said, 'Take out another cigarette'

I obediently took one out; lighted it and after taking 2-3 drags gave it to Ankur, 'No Dude, I have lost my job today itself.'

'F..k!!!!' Ankur said in a shocked voice mixed with the effect of Vodka.

'I don't know what will happen to us when a GOD and a STUD person like you are thrown out of the job. I will never get a job if this thing continues and if stud people like you are thrown out of their job. I also want to have a job in the finance sector as it brings a lot of wealth in such a short time. I wish I crack it like you', Ankur said using all the lingos used in IIT, once again proving that he was an IITian.

He started sharing his own issues and problem in front of me, a lost man.

'It's a financial recession' Rajeev said.

'What's that?' Ankur asked confirming that he didn't even knew F of Finance but had full knowledge of Fs of other words.

Such is today's youth, they want to make money; become powerful in a very short span of time by taking up anything in life which is not even meant for them, or just because few people have reached that height coz of that particular job. But they are ignorant of the financial condition of India.

'Financial instability' I tried to explain it in a layman's language.

'Will I get a job or not?' asked Ankur directly.

'How would I know?' Rajeev said politely.

I was about to speak when Ankur intervened.

Ankur gave a cunning smile and said,' Take out another cigarette'

'This buffoon is here just to have free SUTTAs and Vodka. I have been thrown out of my job and he is crying for his own future which anyways is not going to be that great' I thought in my mind.

He gulped down another bottle of Vodka. I looked by my side to find all the bottles empty. He gave a big smile and asked for another cigarette as if cigarettes were the proteins which would build up his lean body into a macho man.

I had to deny him courteously so that he would leave.

I was having my drink and was trying to reduce my own grief when this fool came and drank up all my spirits.

Finally he stood up and was about to go when suddenly he turned round and finally asked, 'Don't you have any SUTTA, your Majesty'

I laughed at him as it was his favorite dialogue. Even if he found a guy going to the toilet he would pose only one question,' SUTTA hai kya'.

Finally he left in despair as I took my last cigarette out and lighted it.

'Anyways, you didn't tell me about the second surprise' I asked Rajeev with curiosity.

'Oh, yes' Rajeev said with a cunning smile when suddenly his phone rang..

'Here comes her call' Rajeev handed over his handset to me.

My spinning head couldn't recognize the name on the cell and it looked completely blurred.

'Hello, Mr. Banker' the female voice laughed at me.

'Tanya' Rajeev prompted from behind.

'Oh dear, how are you? And you know I am no more a banker' I was taken by a surprise as I didn't expect a call from her. I don't know what to say, friend, beloved or a girl friend.

'Yeah, I know but you will always do something better in your life' Tanya for the first time tried to console me.

'I came to know from Rajeev that you are back in IIT so I called him up to talk to you', she added.

'Yeah, I am back to my alma mater. So you tell me what's happening on your side?' I asked her.

'You know I am still the same, can't we meet tomorrow and talk?' She asked.

I never expected this from a girl who herself broke off the relationship and didn't even bother to talk to me throughout the year and even when I left this place. I thought our relationship had ended.

'Ok, it was your decision not to talk but if you want to meet me again then I will catch up with you near the lake' I said and was about to ring off when she spoke what was on her mind.

'I missed you a lot' she said and rang off.

I couldn't understand what had happened to her suddenly. She knew that I didn't love her but was just attracted to her coz she was the most beautiful girl in IIT.

I came out of my Vodka shots when Rajeev asked about Varun.

'I don't know where he is and I don't even want to know about him' I said furiously.

'I should not enter into your personal matters but I guess you should have sorted out matters between yourselves' Rajeev said which didn't have any effect on me.

'Hey, you go and sleep. You must be having classes tomorrow' I insisted upon Rajeev to leave as I wanted to spend some time alone.

'But JOBS MADE EASY was destined to happen but you all spoiled everything' Rajeev said and left like an obedient junior.

I looked at the calm moon and the sky; closed my eyes. The words of Rajeev haunted me; I took my mobile phone, went into the picture folder and saw snaps of Varun, Vidisha and Tanya, the three people who had gone out of my life.

I was not able to digest my job loss.

'I never expected that one day I will be thrown out of my job. Am I so unlucky?' I asked the divine powers in the sky who were as silent as my dejection.

I closed my eyes to reach back to the scene of my Indian office where my job died today. The gate keeper was still in my mind and in no time my imagination made me reach my office as it had been twelve hours back.

12 hours before: Money Bank Office.

'What happened, where are the rest of the people?', I asked the gate keeper.

'All have left', he said.

'But where?' I inquired from him.

'The bank has been shut down, it has declared its bankruptcy' the cashier said.

'What are you saying? Are you in your senses? I have been sent here from abroad to work and how can it close in one night?" my voice sounded arrogant to the cashier.

'Just see the news and you will get to know what happened exactly', he said.

I was about to enter my office when the few media persons started clicking my photo and thrust the mike in front of me.

'So how are you feeling, Sir?' Some media person asked.

'Did you expect this?' other followed.

'What will you do now?' a few kept on shouting.

'You know you all have ruined the assets of many people who trusted your bank and deposited a lot of money with you' the media guys added to my woes and aggravated my pain.

I didn't have any answer to such a question; I was still to come out of the shock myself.

I didn't bother to answer them and left them only to reach my cabin and find a big lock on the door.

I saw the *chai wala* of our office.

'You know Mr. Banerjee, the investment banker...' he stopped midway.

'He committed suicide yesterday as he has suffered a huge loss on the stock exchange and he knew that he would be thrown out of this job' he said and left.

It was just another shock to me. Mr. Banerjee was a fun loving man. I was in that damn flight when these things happened. It was clear to me that there was lot of panic in the Indian market too. My eyes remained wide open and my ears couldn't believe what they heard.

Finally I reached the T.V room of the office where the news channel reported the debacle of Money Bank.

The news reader on the channel broke a news which shattered my dreams,' Global stock markets plunged on Monday as the dramatic collapse of US investment bank Money Bank sparked steep losses across the financial sector'.

'The collapse of the bank has sent a major jolt through global financial markets as it is by far the biggest victim of the credit crisis that started in August 2007 and had been considered too big to fail', said Global Insight economist Howard Archer.

I left the big office and preferred to wait for some time to come back to my senses. I walked dejectedly down the lanes of Nariman Point and went back into my taxi to reach my room.

Suddenly my sleep, tryst with nostalgia was disturbed by my own chain of thoughts. I struck the bottle with my feet and the empty Vodka bottle rolled down and fell from the 4th floor of the hostel. As it struck the ground it broke into pieces and made me revisit one of the past incidents of my life.

'I walked down the lanes of Hiranandani after having an insatiable debate with my friends. I was not able to walk properly.

Suddenly a speeding car almost ran me over when I shouted from the back in an inebriated state.

"You bloody, can't you see people walking'?" I shouted which didn't have any impact on the driver of the car.

I threw the bottle of wine with all the force I had. It hit the car on the back.

'Now just go' I shouted again.

The speeding car lost its balance and it went on to hit a big tree, the engine caught fire.

'You deserve this' I laughed as the car toppled over.

I turned back, suddenly the glass of the car window broke and a woman was thrown out of it.

She was bleeding profusely. I ran towards her to help.

Back to the reality, on terrace:

Suddenly I rose with blobs of sweat on my face as I tried to forget those past days of my life. I came out of my sleep, took a short stroll on the terrace, tried to abate my anxiety and tried to forget my past. I again closed my eyes and went to sleep as I wanted to end this worst day of my life as soon as possible and make efforts to get a new job and start my life afresh.

It's a new day…new beginning…

My sleep was disturbed by the beam of the hot sun. I came down from the terrace and entered the room. Rajeev was busy on his P.C which I had gifted him after I got placed in the money bank. I hardly gifted anything to anyone but my golden job was enough for me to melt my miser heart.

'Good morning…Dude' I exchanged a smile with Rajeev.

'So, you are still using my computer, I thought you would sell it' I said.

'No, how could I. It was a gift to me, and I believe in cherishing those moments', he said.

'Yeah, but now I am here only' I went for a bath and Rajeev left for his classes.

After having a bath, I came back to the room and after six months or so got busy at my computer once again.

I went to the Documents folder to find certain old files which I had requested Rajiv not to delete. I opened one of those.

'Oh…You were; are and will always be so beautiful Vidisha' I murmured looking at Vidisha's snap in that folder and I kept on looking at some of her snaps.

Finally I opened a folder; it had some snaps of my old days in college when I had joined IIT and Delhi University. Varun was on the screen, just laughing in that picture and beside it was written. 'We have met for life'.

Suddenly I was reminded of Varun, my best friend, but unfortunately our personal differences had made us part. And we had ended the friendship on an acrimonious note, harming both of us as we each lost a companion.

I was reminded of that day when we had clicked this photo. It was just another day in IIT. We went to the lake side, which bordered one side of the IIT campus.

'It's a beautiful place', Varun said.

'Yeah, let's get the boat kept at the shore' I ran towards the boat.

I slipped and went rolling down into the water. Varun started laughing. Rajeev clicked me when I was struggling to come out of the mud laden lake.

'You are looking street smart' Varun said laughingly.

Rajeev clicked this humorous photo of Varun when he was laughing like a kid as he always used to do.

'Oh, those were the best days of my life', I closed that folder containing pictures, opened my mail and downloaded my resume as I was going to start as a fresher.

I saw my brief case which I had left in Rajeev's room; before going; it had all my certificates and degrees.

Finally I opened it and took my resume folder out; it had a layer of dust on it. I cleaned it and in no time I dressed up and was raring to go. I had called the H.R of a finance company and planned to meet him for an interview.

Finally I reached their office.

There was a long queue of students waiting for their turn for the interview. I heaved a huge sigh of relief as I had thought I would be late. The lady at the reception gave me a token which had the number 50 on it. I wondered if any soccer player had that lucky number on his jersey.

'So at what time should I expect my interview' I asked the lady.

'After two hours' she said.

'Oh, long time. I can take a stroll outside and come' I said looking at one of the candidates, waiting for his interview. We exchanged a smile.

I came out of the big office, lighted a cigarette; my only consoler, when that candidate with whom I exchanged a smile came up from behind.

'So, I guess you are also last in the big queue.' I said to him.

'Yeah' he lighted his own cigarette.

'An organization is like a tree full of monkeys, all on different limbs at different levels. Some monkeys climbing up, some down. The monkey on top looks down; see a tree full of smiling faces. The monkey on the bottom looks up; sees only assholes and licks them to reach the top.' The young guy shared his views.

'True' I complemented him.

'So are you an experienced candidate or a fresher?' I asked him.

'No, I am a fresher' he said and wanted to know the same from me.

'Yeah, I could have been an experienced candidate but when everything was going fine, I was thrown out of the Money Bank.' I breathed out my cigarette.

'Oh, so you were working in that bank then you will definitely crack this job since Money Bank only takes the crème de la crème of students', he said to me, which boosted my confidence, which has sunk 20 meters down into the earth.

'Let's see what happens. I have witnessed one of the most surprising phases of my life so I don't expect anything now' I said and we started moving towards the lobby.

'But I want this job; I have a family to support. I have very limited means' he suddenly spoke. He probably belonged to a poor family and wanted to support his family and his ailing mom.

'Don't worry you will get a job. Seeing the number of applications, I guess there are a good number of openings in the company' I said to give this stranger some confidence which had sunk even lower than mine.

'Only ONE' he said it loudly.

I preferred to keep quiet since I knew I could be one of those who could be axed here also, just like two nights back when I was thrown out of my own job. We entered the H.R office.

Finally my turn came and I went inside for my interview. My interview went well as always and all the candidates waited for the result. Finally the receptionist displayed the result on the notice board of the company.

One of the candidates peeped in first and jumped after seeing the result, he was ecstatic. I understood he had got the job, so I left as I knew that the company was looking for only one potential candidate. I was frustrated at this moment, as I had thought it was a lollypop for a potential candidate like me.

I came out of the office and was about to take an autoricksaw when I saw the candidate with whom I had talked before my interview. His eyes were full of tears and he walked dejectedly. I didn't try to give him solace as I was unable to recover from my own shock. I reached IIT to find Tanya sitting in Rajeev's room.

'Hey how are you my sweetu...?' she said.

'Hey, don't call me by that name. I hate that word' I said angrily on hearing that feminine word.

'Ok, ok. So just tell me how are you? How was your interview?' She asked.

'I am trying to get a job and have got rejected in one' I said keeping my laptop and resumé folder on the desk.

'You have gained some weight but still you look smart' she remarked.

'But you are still gorgeous and sexy as ever' I blinked my eyes looking on her lips which looked like strawberries.

She reciprocated my statement with a deceptive womanly smile.

'What have you brought for me from the United States?' she asked as she frantically kept on looking here and there searching for some kind of gift which she expected from me.

I didn't know what happened to this girl, she went out of the relationship because she wanted commitment and she knew that I never loved her that way. But now suddenly she has changed a lot. It was her decision not to talk; now she was as friendly as ever.

'I have brought nothing, I have been thrown out of my job and you are expecting a damn gift from me' I said loudly.

She was hurt and her face dropped.

'I am so sorry, actually I am not in my senses after my debacle and even today I didn't manage a job' I said with a low voice.

'You will get one soon, don't worry' She kissed my cheeks.

She was behaving in a very different manner. A kiss from her was the last thing which I expected.

'Let's go out for a movie' she said.

I thought a movie would be relaxing for me in such a tough situation and we went for a Bollywood flick.

'When you want something, the entire universe conspires in helping you to achieve it' said Shahrukh Khan, the King Khan in his magnum opus OM SHANTI OM. Tanya appreciated the dialogue.

'*BAKWAAS* (RUBBISH)' I thought. If that had been the case I would have never lost my job and definitely not Vidisha.

Finally the movie full of turns and twists, incarnations got over, a typical Bolly movie. We decided to have coffee.

'So what happened? You have changed suddenly. You never wanted to talk to me but now I am witnessing a transformation' I fired my queries immediately.

She thought a lot, looked here and there and finally spoke, 'You know some relationships should not be given a name. When we stopped talking I realized that we were always good friends'

'But keep these things aside, you tell me now what's on your card' she changed the topic of discussion.

'Well, I will try out some new jobs and if nothing clicks I will go for a PhD program in Europe' I said to her.

'Hmmm...Good planning', she appreciated my plans.

Finally we reached back to the IIT; I escorted her to the girls' hostel; one of the sought after places by many guys and finally reached my room. Rajeev was preparing his own resumé for the coming placements in December.

'Ohhh..So you are planning for a job in this turbulent environment' I said to him.

'Who doesn't want to have one?' he said with a cunning smile.

I ended my hectic day by going off to sleep. I opened my eyes to look at the TIMES OF INDIA newspaper which said, 'What started as a purely US investment bank problem has slowly spread to the entire financial sector across the world. And now it is engulfing entire economies. There is a consensus that the world is rushing headlong into a prolonged recession. Columnists remind us of the Great Depression, when US real economic output fell by a third between 1929 and 1933, unemployment rose from 3 to 25 per cent and stock markets took twenty five years to regain their peak. There is a danger of governments tightening public spending or raising tariff barriers, thereby risking a deep recession.'

I came out of my dream world and realised that this financial crisis is going to be a bit longer than expected. I turned on a few pages to look at the news on the financial turbulence.

'India's stock exchange has seen drastic fall in the index. SENSEX have touched the lowest point ever. There is a fear of FINANCIAL RECESSION in India too' the article said.

For the next few days such articles were common and were cited as everyday news in all the newspapers.

'Huge job losses in all sectors, companies laying off many employees, few companies closing down' was becoming common news.

I applied to many companies irrespective of their openings and without knowing their exact functioning.

'A single job was always better than having no job and that single job could be anything!' I always thought like this.

I opened accounts in all the online job portals and websites. I registered myself in all. I didn't think, even a week ago, that I was going to land in such a huge problem.

Suddenly from nowhere I typed, 'www.jobsmadeeasy.com'.

'Page not found or error in construction' message came on the screen.

Rajeev entered the room and I quickly closed the internet tab.

For the next few days, I was busy in appearing for all sorts of interviews. But unfortunately I couldn't crack any one of them. I was CRIPPLED like many others.

♥

It was Tanya's birthday. I called to wish her.

'Let's meet tomorrow in the evening, we will party' she said in her jolly mood.

'Ok' I said as I wanted to come out of my present life which was only full of failures and gloominess.

I left my room and went out for jogging.

There was complete panic in the institution with students speculating whether any company would come for recruitment in campus or not. So powerful was the impact of the recession.

'I thought I wanted a career; turns out I just wanted paycheques.' I thought as I crossed the Gymnasium.

I had hardly covered a mile when I recognized the back of the person who was running in front of me.

I covered the distance between us by running faster and catching up with him.

'VARUN....YOU.........' I said with some hiccups in my voice.

He was also astonished to see me too.

'Yeah, I just came here to my friends to have a good weekend' he said.

'I heard your bank has been shut down, so what are you planning next?' Varun sounded like a thorough professional. Probably nothing was left in our friendship.

I still remember when we used to meet after a long period, we would hug each other; exchange smiles but probably time had changed now, and we were harmless but inimical.

'Let's see, I will get something in this hard time too' I said confidently not exposing my grief.

'Where are you these days?' I inquired from him.

'Yeah, I am happy as an engineer in a steel company' he said.

'I didn't know whether to take it as a comment, or harsh words' I thought.

I smiled as I realized that our friendship has ended after JOBSMADEEASY.

'People take job without any interest in a particular field.' Varun murmured. 'This is what happens to people who take hasty decision.'

'I have saved enough money in three months only which a steel company offers in a year.' I replied harshly.

'Anyways who cares, people are happy there and are secured.' Varun started an insatiable discussion. I didn't want to enter in it.

I remained quiet and didn't reply. It became clear to us that we could not stand each other for more than 5 minutes, once a life time buddy.

'OK, Bye. I will catch up with you some other time' Varun showed some courtesy and left. Varun and I used to go miles for early morning joggings but today we were unable to walk even a few meters together.

It hardly bothered me and I continued on my way and I was pretty sure that it would not have bothered him too.

I purchased some fresh flowers for Tanya which she liked. Suddenly after coming here my past was haunting me. I met some persons who were special in my life, after coming here. I reached my room; took a bath and started filling out lot of off campus job forms which was the most important work at this point for me.

'Oh God, its 7.00 pm' I looked at my watch and finally rushed to the main gate where Tanya was waiting for me.

• She took me to MAINLAND CHINA, a Chinese restaurant located at Hiranandani; our favorite hangout.

I presented the flowers to her; she looked stunning in black. She had a perfect figure with a beautiful face and smile.

'Oh..So you still remember my choices' she said, looking at the yellow flowers.

I was reminded of Rajeev's dialogue and I said it in one go, 'Just as a failed candidate cannot forget the subject in which he failed until he has failed in many, just as a horse cannot forget his grasses and just as a tube light cannot forget the electric current which runs it, in the same way how can I forget you and your taste my friend?' I myself felt it was a pure comical dialogue.

She laughed as we entered the restaurant. It was an undoubtedly clear feeling from my side that she was my good friend.

'Let's have some Chinese food today', she said.

'Why not, it's your birthday, you can have whatever you want', I smiled as we entered the restaurant.

People can be so superstitious. The owner of the restaurant kept watching at the news channel which was showing a special program on RECESSION—my nightmare.

The name of that episode was RECESSION PROOF BABA.

The news reporter was sitting beside a Brahmin who had self proclaimed himself as a RECESSION PROOF BABA and had catapulted to stardom over night.

I came to know about the whole story as I was reminded of the case which was captured in the national news.

The article mentioned about a Brahmin who had guided a merchandiser to a hell lot of profit. He asked him to buy the stocks of a company which was not performing well for the last few weeks. And to everyone's surprise the index of the stock of the company rose that resulted in a lot of wealth to the merchandiser. I wished if that could have been the case with Mr. Smith having discussion with the *baba*.

And this Brahmin who used to sit in front of our main gate was catapulted to new heights. He suddenly became a superstar and center of attraction and got a new name and a new brand.

'Let's see how the RECESSION PROOF BABA makes a decision or chooses a stock in such turbulent times' the reporter on the channel shouted to catch the attention of as many people as possible.

Tanya laughed as we peeped into the television set.

'Bacchha (My Son).........' Said the Brahmin loudly putting a tilak on the forehead of the reporter and shouted as if P.C Sarkar was carrying on his magic shows.

Everyone in the restaurant looked at the television set, even a few people from outside peeped inside the A.C restaurant.

The Baba closed his eyes and kept on enchanting some prayers which everyone could make to be a mélange of Gayatri mantra, Hanuman chalisa and a part of Bhawgad Gita in a language that was neither complete Hindi nor complete English. I was bemused to see how people were made fools of. Finally he lighted a few incense sticks and lighted a camphor tablet in his hand; showed it to goddess Laxmi.

'Look at the fraud' Tanya said to me.

'Still I appreciate this man, he is making money even in this time of recession when big business have failed' I replied.

'But he is making everyone around him…'

'A FOOL' I completed Tanya's sentence. But it's official in business and you carry on until you are caught.

Finally the Baba took some papers in his hand, rolled out some dices and added all the numbers on the dices and finally opened his laptop. He matched the total number on the dices with few words and then he came up with an answer. I never thought Baba to be a techno-savvy one.

'Probably he is calculating some probability and stocks volatility' I said laughingly.

'Now, I guess you have to learn some investment tips from the recession proof Baba' Tanya made a comment and made me realized that finance was not my cup of tea but I chose it just for the sake of money. I too accepted it with a heavy heart since I was unsuccessful at getting a job locally and lost one globally.

'Finally after some manipulations, out of three companies he chose one; giving the media a properly framed answer for his choice which was a jargon of its own kind which hardly anyone could comprehend. He ordered the reporter to compare the stock index of that company with its closing price'

'The index has risen' said the reporter cross checking with the index of the market.

The people standing by the side of the RECESSION PROOF BABA started touching his feet and started chanting his name.

'Bachcha, aaj invest karo isme aur faal khao.........Jiyo jee bhar ke....' he said loudly.

'My child, invest you money today in this and enjoy the fruit and enjoy your life to the fullest' the Baba repeated with full confidence.

From nowhere a man in rags rose, decided to make a fool of everyone and earned a lot of money and started his business of financial advisory.

Finally he sat in his huge king size throne; his followers lifted the throne and went away. His followers chased him. He was becoming a craze for many.

'So today's mantra is to buy the stock of TECHNOfront and see your money growing' Sushil Pandey reporting from Baba's den in Delhi.

Tanya almost spitted out the coke as she tried to control her laughter.

'The world needs Babas like this and no investment bankers like us' I exchanged a smile with Tanya.

Finally we ordered the sumptuous food.

'You are looking really beautiful' I appreciated Tanya's beauty.

She blushed.

Finally I ordered some beer, Tanya surprised me when she showed signs of drinking it for the first time.

After having a decent volume of beer, we decided to check out. We were walking on the road.

Tanya walked in a zig zag manner; probably she had taken more beer than her capacity. I held her hands and shoulder; she leaned on me. We took a taxi as there was no auto to be seen. 'Take me with you, I want to be away from my hostel today, else I will be caught at the gate of my hostel and severe penalty will be imposed on me if I am caught drunk.' She said as I felt the fragrance of a woman. I wondered how she could think so far, when she was not even able to walk.

I called Rajeev and narrated to him the entire story and requested him to sleep in some other room.

I took Tanya out of the auto; the next challenge was to make a girl enter into a boy's hostel at night. I lifted her in my arms, she almost slept. She looked damn beautiful and irresistibly attractive. I jumped the wall with Tanya in my arms. Her fragrance filled my breath; she was so close to me that we could feel each other's breath; a perfect close-up breath freshness advertisement could be filmed.

Finally I somehow managed to bring her to Rajeev's room. I opened his room with my master key. And I closed the door.

Tanya opened her eyes, pulled me towards her and kissed my cheeks. I held her arms and kept on looking in her eyes. Suddenly my past and my present appeared in her eyes. I saw Varun, Vidisha and Vinod's faces in those beautiful eyes. She held me with her arms around me; she closed her eyes and slowly brought her lips near mine.

'What am I doing' I said to myself as I closed my arms and Tanya was in between them. 'I always wanted to be cozy with her.' I said to myself as her lips just touched mine.

I pulled my self back and lifted my arms to release myself from her arms. I moved out and made her sit on the bed.

She asked,' Why?'

Probably she knew I always wanted this from her without any commitment.

'I can't do this with you, sorry' I said and left the room and called Rajeev to escort Tanya to her hostel.

It was 2 am; the night was dusky and roads were empty. I started running; I didn't know why I was running. Was I running from my past or was I running away from my present?

I reached near the lake side. I took some deep breathes; sat down on a bench near the shore of the lake. Suddenly my past was in front of me, my life long friendship with Varun, Vinod, the only love of the life…Vidisha and our JOBS MADE EASY.

I lighted my cigarette, looked at the calm sky. Tears started rolling down my cheeks, this was the first time I had shed tear on my personal and career losses.

'Who am I? What am I doing? Where will I land up after three or four years? I have been a loser throughout my life; lost a job; lost my love; lost lifelong friends and one day will lose my life. Does merit have no standing in the market; will everyone get a job when the market is in boom? Is talent not recession proof? Who am I? What am I doing? Whatever happened to me was the worst thing which could have happen to anyone but I will not allow it to happen to my friends, family. I will fight against all odds. But what can I do? I wish I had not thrown the bottle on the car last night.' I closed my eyes and suddenly I started visualizing some faces and I reached my past. I was really in a predicament and wished to come out of it.

When love and friendship struck...

Some four small years back...

'I LOVE YOU......' I said to Vidisha.

Vidisha blushed and in no time the sound reached every corner of the classroom.

'SMACK....................' Vidisha's hand made a perfect contact with my cheeks; making carbon print of her soft hands.

Vidisha was my senior in Hindu College, Delhi University.

'It's just ragging' few seniors told Vidisha.

I felt embarrassed and I left the class. I was really dejected since ragging is the introductory period of one's college life.

'We were just having fun and a small ragging session when you slapped this poor junior' Vidisha was made to feel guilty by her friends.

I reached the canteen, I splashed some water on my face and looked in the mirror just to check whether the finger prints had been erased from my cheeks or not.

'It was a nice shot' a voice interrupted.

I exchanged a smile with this simple looking guy.

'Yeah, it was just like Tendulkar's cover drive right from the middle of the bat' I blinked my eyes at this person showing my expertise at the game's religion whose God's name I had mentioned in my statement.

'Hi, I am Varun' he said.

'I am Armaan and nice to meet you' I courteously shook his hand.

'But anyways you are lucky, you got a chance to propose to the most beautiful girl in college' Varun said with a smiling face.

'Yeah, but it was just ragging'.

'Don't worry, you never know; may be its destined to happen this way' Varun said smilingly in SRK fashion.

We went to the hostel.

'Oh..yeah....' a female voice rang through the silence of the corridor.

'Yeah..Come on....' the voice soon became seducing.

'Ahhh......Ahhh.....' we reached near the door from where the sound was coming.

Some senior was getting intimate with his girl friend.

We tried to peep in and Varun raised me on his shoulders.

'Just a bit more' I said to Varun.

'I can't, you are a giant' he said pointing to my extra pounds.

I was just about to have a live telecast of the ding dong going inside when Varun couldn't bear my weight and I toppled over him.

The movements inside the room stopped as a strong vehement voice made us panic.

'Who is there?' the voice said.

We rushed towards our room; Varun left his spectacles and ran away.

I went inside the toilet and hid myself.

After some time, Varun and I reached our room. I was surprise to find Varun as my new room mate.

After that incident; that senior was always seen with Varun's spectacles in his hand inquiring from others about the owner of the optical object.

'Hey where are your specs?' the senior suspiciously asked Varun.

Varun hesitantly looked at me and said 'I have forgotten it in my lab.'

The senior looked with a suspicious eye.

But somehow we managed to escape from there.

'Why don't you buy a new one' I said to him.

'I will buy it, but if this insidious senior comes to know that the specs are mine. He would kill me' Varun said.

'Don't worry; he will never come to know. There are so many people in the hostel who wear specs and anyways your spectacles were too old and had a circular frame. Let's try something cool and trendy this time' I suggested to Varun.

We went to Connaught Place to buy a pair of specs for Varun. For the first time we tasted whisky.

Varun behaved like a sober man even after three pegs of Royal Stag but it was more than enough for me to bring my mischievous nature out.

'Hey, I wish I too had a girl friend' I said to Varun.

"You can have more than one. I am pretty sure of this, you are good looking and moreover better than that senior too who knows the art of having girls go gaga over men' Varun raised me to the sky.

'Look at that senior, he is so dark complexioned and has the body of an elephant. But still he manages girl and directs them to his bed' I said while we were taking a stroll in the C.P garden.

'But he has something which matters a lot' Varun said.

'MONEY' Girls go gaga over it.

I will have a girl soon.

'Vidisha will be quite good for you' Varun reminded me of the slap.

I touched my cheeks to check whether all my teeth were intact as I was sure the carbon prints were all over.

'But she is not my type.'

'And what's your type of girl?' he asked.

'It can be any one who doesn't believe in commitments.' My answer was more than clear to Varun.

After purchasing new specs we came back to the hostel.

As we entered the gate, we found that senior again.

He noticed Varun's specs.

'Good' he said and left thinking that the specs he had found were Varun's.

"The WIKIPEDIA" the starting tag which was given to Varun, a person with a great heart, and a true friend in real sense, the boy had a great wealth of knowledge and there was a charm in the way he explained his answers. He was a simple natured boy from a small town, who believed in dreaming tall. His etiquette attire gives a feel that he is a screwed manager who always offers lucrative deals. He was lean and thin but had a lot of energy stored in him. And in a very short time he became my close friend and the friendship started to caste its magic on us.

Classes got over and I came out of the class to find Vidisha standing in the corridor.

She exchanged a smile and came near me.

I was reminded of the last day when she had slapped me. I rubbed my hand on my cheeks still facing the frictional heat and having the experience of law of conservation of energy.

She smiled and said 'Don't worry. I will do nothing'

I exchanged a smile with this beautiful face.

'Let's move to the canteen' she appeared friendly today.

The lustful feelings surrounded my mind like the cloud surrounding the blue sky. I gave a small smile to the students sitting in the corridor; they gave a tough look as if I was dating their sister. Vidisha was one of the few beautiful girls with brain present in the college.

'I am sorry for the last day, actually I don't like all such stupid acts, but it was not your fault too as you were caught in the midst of a ragging' Vidisha said in her soft voice.

She started the conversation.

'It's OK. I know you did it unintentionally' I moved to the canteen counter to place the order. The guys at the canteen were looking at her with hungry eyes.

After all I have to accept the fact that men are dog and they never miss a chance to have a look on a beautiful lady; even some try to impress them by something which looks foolish. I thought.

And for the first time I observed Vidisha with my inner eyes as she looked here and there while I was placing the order.

It was not like I had never seen such a beautiful girl before. Her beauty was divine, with no make up her beauty glowed like a flower. Her long curls were blowing in the air. Her beautiful eyes were like the deep sea in which everyone would like to take a plunge. Her smile was inimitable. The red top only added to her beauty. Her eyes were expressive and her smile had divine power to make even a drooping flower bloom, a dying man to come back to his senses. Her smile could control all the powers of nature. She had a white complexion, lips like pink petals of a rose and expressive eyes.

I was getting attracted to her and wanted to launch a big hug and kisses but somehow I kept my hormones dormant.

I almost fell over while coming back, that was the power of her beauty. I remembered John Keats who had said,' Truth is beauty and the beauty is truth' and the well known fact that Truth is the ultimate power. So the power of beauty did topple me.

'So where are you from?' she asked me.

We introduced each other.

'I am from Jampot and what about you?' I asked.

She looked with a wrinkled face, 'Is that in India?'

"Yes, it's in Jharkhand and is more famous as Jamshedpur.' The abbreviation made by some modern people of Jharkhand was difficult for most of the people to comprehend.

She started laughing.

"Is there anything to laugh?' I asked her.

'Jampot sounds quite funny......'She kept on giggling.

Many unknown faces of college came to me and asked about my whereabouts, they just came to check in the girl with whom I was sitting. Even my enemies came to say good afternoon just to have a glimpse of this beautiful lady.

'Well I am from Himachal' she said sipping her cappuccino. I still wonder why girls prefer cappuccino to coffee.

'I guess the state is quite big' we exchanged a smile.

'I am from Kullu' she said..

'Ahhh.....' I cried in agony.

'What happened?' she inquired.

I pressed my cheeks with hand while sipping coffee, which reminded her of the slap. It was just to make her realize her deed.

'I am so sorry for that' she said with all innocence in her eyes.

'No, it's OK' I said laughingly.

'So if you have any problem in college or you need any notes, any guidance, then feel free to contact me' Vidisha behaved like a generous senior.

'Should I ask her for her mobile number?' I kept on thinking as it was just the first meeting. There was a cold war going between my mind and my brain.

'So let's move' she was about to move.

'But you have a lot of strength; your slap was too powerful. It could have easily knocked out a few teeth of mine' I laughed pointing to her slim personality.

'Oh..I am so sorry for that. Don't make me feel guilty anymore' Vidisha said. I saw real innocence in her eyes.

'Should I take her mobile number?' the cloud of questions again hovered around my mind.

But it was too late; she had gone inside her class after waving at me.

'Ohh...She is really pretty.' I said to Varun as the lecturer tried to explain the concept of electromagnetic theory.

'So where were you?' Varun asked me.

'With Vidisha' I smiled.

My voice reached the ears of the lecturer and we were thrown out of the class and we were really very happy.

Varun even said "Thank you" to the professor.

'Let's sit in the canteen and talk, it was difficult to talk in between that boring lecture' I smiled.

'Rightly said, it's good that we have been thrown out of the class, now we can enjoy for one hour' Varun said.

I was sitting in the canteen with Varun when a message appeared on my cell. It was another message from Vodafone.

'Live Chat' the title of the message.

The message said, '*Make new friends and date online. For Priya(21) type P, for Ria(19) type R, for Gary (20) type G and for Mitali(19) type M and send it to 99999*'

Varun advised me to try out for girls with the age of 19.

'Hi..This is Armaan from Delhi' I quickly typed a message for R and M and sent it on the given number.

'So, today you will get one girl finally' Varun told me.

I laughed and kept on checking my mobile. But no one replied, no surprises. I knew my luck.

I think these telecom people think that we are fools and we would waste our money like this. That's why they keep on giving new offers.

'No, this is not the case; your message must have reached someone, may be to the call center girl who will fool you and probably she will reply and make you reply too, benefitting the Vodafone service' Varun said finishing his kebab roll.

'Yeah, a tight slap was not enough for me, now I will start wasting my money soon' I said.

We moved to the hostel. Days passed, I used to meet Vidisha almost every day, exchange a smile and a few words but still I didn't don enough courage to ask her number. Exams were coming near. Varun and I made night outs and arranged notes to pass the exams.

I made it a point to visit Vidisha's paying guest room daily to get my doubts cleared. Who wanted to get the doubt clear, I just wanted to see her beautiful face.

After the exams Varun took me to his home in Faridabad. He had an ailing father who was recovering from lung cancer. I was astonished when Varun told me this; he never looked discomforted in front of me and was going through this trauma alone. These smiling faces can obscure many dark secrets.

'Good morning uncle' I touched Varun's father's feet.

He didn't say much and made a few gestures in the air like a Chinese athlete performing martial arts.

From his gesture I understood that he blessed me.

Varun sat beside his father, a retired lecturer. I sat in front of the two.

'Why has this happened to him?' I asked Varun about his father's health.

'Excessive smoking' a female voice interrupted us. It was Varun's mother.

'How many times have I told him, CIGARETTE SMOKING IS DANGEOUS FOR HEALTH. But why would he listen to me' her voice almost shrank and eyes got moistened.

'Leave it Mom, now nothing can be changed' Varun insisted upon his mother not to cry.

She kept the cups of tea in front of us and some biscuits and left.

Varun took the tea and raised his father on his arms from the rest chair. His father started sipping the tea.

Varun was a real hero, a great son, a very good friend and above all A GREAT HUMAN BEING.

Finally he helped his father to have a cup of tea.

I started sipping mine.

'It happened six months back. Dad was having a continuous pain in his chest Initially he didn't bother but at last when he went to the doctor, the doctor told him that he had lung cancer due to excessive smoking' Varun said bravely.

'Smoking can really be fatal, but people smoke just for the sake of fun and style' I said to him without realizing what harm it would inflict on me as I was getting addicted to it.

Finally Varun took me to his room. The room looked like Einstein's lab, full of books, walls pasted with articles on science and lots of educational C.Ds.

'It seems you study a lot.' I had to make a remark after seeing his room. I could easily make out the difference between a hell and a heaven. My room certainly looked like hell, it had all the things which could attract a normal male but after entering into it; he would definitely turn into an evil.

'No, I used to do that once but after my father's condition, things aren't in right shape' Varun said turning on his personal computer.

Yeah, I can understand. I went near his laptop, lifted one C.D. It was a video of Ratan Tata giving a speech on ENTREPRENEURSHIP'

So, you want to be an Entrepreneur?

'Who doesn't want to have his own business?' Varun replied.

I nodded my head in unison. Varun was determined.

'Hey I have a DVD of Quantum of Solace, you wanna see it?' Varun asked me,

Why not? James Bond is my favorite onscreen character.

Varun's mom brought some pop corn and mango shake for us. We completed the movie in two hours and were about to leave.

Varun's mother was sitting beside his father and was making him eat his liquid food and was cursing him that he didn't behave like a responsible man and just threw away his life without caring for the family.

'Stop Ma…'Varun said.

I thought Varun was feeling uncomfortable because of me. I also felt awkward and didn't want to enter into his family affairs. I left the room and waited outside his dilapidated house.

'No more now' I took a cigarette packet from my pocket, crushed it in my hand and threw it away.

'It drags your life out of you; believe me, it does it very slowly, prolonging your death' Varun suddenly came from behind.

Yeah, I was just having fun. But I never thought of the consequences; not knowing that I would start smoking again very soon. These things are like a candle flame; a moth knows that it will burn itself but it still goes near the flame as it is attracted by it.

I hugged Varun for the first time; he was definitely a great chap and a great son. I was really lucky to have such a guy as my friend.

We reached back to our room in the hostel.

♥

A message appeared on my mobile. I was surprised to see the message.

Varun, there is a message from Mitali (19), remember her. My voice was full of excitement and passionate like a teenager having sex for the first time.

'Y..Yeah...I guess Vodafone one' he said.

Yeah..She has written, 'Hi...I am Mitali Saxena and I live in Delhi and study in Delhi University."

'See, she has given you the entire address. What are you waiting for? Just start messaging. You never know you can be like one of those seniors who put their girl friends on the bed.' Varun said to me making me feel on top of the 7th floor.

'Hi, I am also living in this campus' I messaged Mitali.

And in no time another message came on my mobile.

'Hey, I am going to T.V room, you continue with your SMS romance' Varun left.

'Hi, nice to hear from you again. Can we be friends?' her message said.

Am I looking like a fool who will not accept a friend request from a girl? I thought.

'Yeah, why not after all we are neighbors and one should love thy neighbor' I typed the message.

She replied the message with a smile, 'J'

Then started the usual buzz; we introduced each other, shared some jobs, our hobbies and stuff like that.

'Good night dear, I will talk to you tomorrow' another message came instantly.

I slept too. I got attracted to Mitali just by receiving a few messages from her. How infatuated was I?

I reached college to find my seniors and a few friends celebrating the birthday of Vidisha. It was 5th January.

I also joined them. Her friend rubbed the cake cream on her face. I felt jealous when few of her friends of the opposite sex did it.

I felt perturbed and I left that place.

'Hey, where are you going' Vidisha asked from behind.

'Class' I said and continued towards my class room.

Suddenly I received a message on my mobile; I opened it thinking it to be from Mitali. But it was a message from a new number.

'I am so sorry; I think you are still angry with me. Can I take you for a movie on my special day....Vidisha' I was astonished to see Vidisha's message. She probably managed my number from Varun. I didn't realize how lucky I was.

'I am not angry, I would definitely join you on your special day and indeed make this day very special for you' I replied and finally I got Vidisha's mobile number.

'THANKs.I will catch you at the metro station' her reply came quickly.

'So suddenly you have two girls in your life, one is your senior and the other a junior.' Varun said with a big smile.

My choice will be tough. I exchanged a smile with him.

'Why don't we meet today evening in the rose garden?' I read Mitali's message which came in between the class.

'Today I am going for a movie, can we meet tomorrow?' I replied.

'MOVIE without me, Can I join you?' Mitali asked.

I didn't know why she sounded so possessive, she hardly knew me.

'No, Sorry. I am going on a birthday treat. I will definitely catch you tomorrow, my sweet new friend' I added the adjective.

She didn't reply, I thought she was angry but I didn't bother to ask her as I was going for a movie with the most beautiful girl of our college, every man's dream girl.

I reached near the metro station fifteen minutes before as I was too anxious to go with her.

Finally the birthday girl came in a beautiful pink suit which blew my heart away. She was looking like a goddess; she had applied some *kajol* to her eyes and those eyes were looking really beautiful and expressive. She smiled as she saw me, and started walking towards me. Her face was shining brilliantly; looked like an angel from heaven. Her long hair was coming in front of her eyes and was irritating her. She put it across but the mischievous hair wanted to kiss her eyes just like my lips who wanted to make contact to those soft and beautiful lips.

'You look damn beautiful' I thought of saying it.

'Hey, what are you hiding?' she asked me and brought me out of my dreams.

'Nothing' I said.

She behaved like just any other girl and not like a senior.

When you try to hide something from a girl they will never let you get off so easily. I gave up hiding it.

'Ohh...beautiful flowers' her eyes remained wide open.

'This bouquet is for you.' I said trying to copy expressions of Shahrukh Khan.

'Thanks, these white and yellow flowers are my favorite' Vidisha said.

'But these flowers are not as beautiful as you' I again tried a Bollywood dialogue to impress her.

She didn't even blush; a deadly weapon to impress any guy but I didn't expect such a lukewarm response from her.

I thought she would instantaneously hug me and would kiss me hard.

'Hey hold my bag' she said.

'ANYTHING FOR YOU MA'AM' I said risibly.

For the first time, she blushed. I looked up at the sky and said to the heavenly powers dwelling in heaven. 'THANK YOU'.

We reached the PVR and bought tickets for HUM TUM.

I thought this title would be more suitable for me and finally I donned some courage and said, looking into Vidisha's eyes, 'HUM TUM' I played my strokes.

'Hey, let's go inside the hall, I don't want to miss the starting of this movie' she said.

My attempt to impress her went in vain as she didn't understand or didn't want to express her feeling.

She was an ardent Bollywood fan and appreciated its songs.

She went on enjoying the movie while I sat there only to see her.

Suddenly from nowhere she started singing the title track of the movie, HUM TUM on seeing Saif Ali Khan romancing with Bollywood queen, Rani Mukherjee.

'Saanson Ko Saanson Mein Dalne Do Zara'.

'*Dheemi Si Dhadkan Ko Badne Do Zara'* she sang it perfectly

'*Lamho Ki Guzarish Hai Yeh Paas Aa Jaaye*' I followed her, she looked at me; gave a beautiful smile. I played my stroke.

'*Hum...Hum.....Tum...*' she sang along with Rani Mukherjee.

'*Tum... Hum Tum...*' I sang looking at Vidisha.

I thought I had fired my gun. But again it didn't have any impact on Vidisha.

She just complemented the entire song.

Finally the movie got over. Vidisha kept on praising the movie. I took Vidisha to Haldiram's in Moolchand.

'You have a very good voice' I complemented her soft voice.

'You too.' she said.

Finally we ordered Indian food.

'I am so sorry for that slap, I guess you are still angry with me' Vidisha said to me.

'Not at all' I replied and I asked her to forget about it.

'Then why did you leave when I was cutting the cake?' she asked.

'I had a class' I defended my act.

'But Varun was seen roaming, he said that there was a break' Vidisha said.

I didn't have any answer now. I myself didn't know why I had left the place. Was I jealous when the boys were putting cake on Vidisha? But why?

I tried to change the conversation.

'You called me today because you are still feeling guilty. If you had told me that you wanted to take me for a treat on your birthday. I would have been much happier.

'I didn't mean that by my message' she said.

'Then Sorry Madam; I also couldn't understand your message.'

I don't want that people should sympathize to me; it will not work with me. I don't want to be just another guy in your life. I couldn't keep a control on my mouth. She looked suspiciously, I kept quiet.

'I never go out with any boys; some have approached me too. But I maintain a good distance from them. But after meeting you, I thought you were quite decent and a simple guy as compared to my other friends. So I thought we can be good friends; and obviously I wanted to say sorry to you' Vidisha said.

My eyes remained wide open. I couldn't believe my luck, one of the most beautiful girls in the college wished to have friendship with me.

It's really amazing how a girl can change ones ferocious anger into love and they can do it just by a smile or few soft words.

'Friends' I brought my hand forward to shake Vidisha's hand.

'Good friends' she added the adjective.

And in a very short span of time, we became good friends. She asked about me, my hobbies and my background. I asked her the same and came to know about her secrets, part time hobby and what she liked the most.

We preferred to take a stroll before taking a taxi.

The road was lit up with moonlight and it appeared more illuminated because of the divine beauty beside me.

She kept on observing things near the road and became ecstatic on seeing a beautiful garden in front of us. She really looked beautiful which was as natural as the flowers in the garden with no artificial stuff in it.

'Am I falling for her?' a question came to my mind.

She gave a beautiful look and we proceeded towards the garden.

'Have I started liking her?'

I myself didn't know the answer.

'Hey should I say something?' I finally had the courage.

Vidisha asked suspiciously, 'WHAT?'

You are looking beautiful; I must say you are really sweet.

'Thanks' she blushed as was her usual habit.

I have a gift for you, and you know I am lucky too.

'Another gift?' she smiled.

Seriously, one thing was missing in you today. And I think my gift will complete it.

I took from my pocket, ARCHIES ear rings which I had brought for her.

'Oh, they're so beautiful. 'She said.

Look at the color of your dress, the pink color ear rings will match with your dress.

'It would be too expensive' she said, looking at the rings.

'It's meant only for good friends' finally my last dialogue impressed her.

'But good friends don't give the gift this way' she said, which left me puzzled.

She stood by my side, lifted the hair near her ear and said , 'PUT IT ON.'

I smiled and took those ear rings and put them on her ear. I could feel the fragrance of a woman. She smiled while I was putting the rings on her ears.

Finally we left for the hostel; I escorted her to her P.G (paying guest room).

'Thanks for the special day' I said to her; since the memoirs of the day would always be cherished by me.

She gave a smile and said, 'Thanks for the special gift and the priceless moments'.

I reached the hostel to find six missed calls from Mitali. I tried to call her back. But she didn't pick up her phone; probably she had got angry as I neglected her.

I was not able to understand my own feelings for the first time.

'Hey, how was your evening? I guess it must have been good. After all you were with the most beautiful girl.' Varun said risibly.

My smile said it all to Varun.

'I will not talk to you, I tried your phone but you didn't give any response' Mitali's message came in suddenly.

I called her and this time she picked up the phone, 'Hi, I am sorry. I was so busy that I couldn't take your cell. I will meet you tomorrow.'

She smiled, the voice was seducing, 'Well, no problem. I will catch up with you tomorrow at the park.'

Then she started talking about her, her likes etc.

'What are you doing man?' Varun said as I ended Mitali's call.

'You have spent so much time today with Vidisha and tomorrow you will be with Mitali. I am not able to understand what's going on with you' Varun was equally puzzled.

I also couldn't understand. Was this the way every teenager behaves or am I getting equally attracted towards the two ladies? With such a chain of thoughts I started listening to some Rock songs and dozed off.

It was just another morning; Vidisha saw me and joined me at lunch in the canteen.

'So, I hope you enjoyed the movie yesterday' she said.

I enjoyed a lot. I said as I kept on observing that beautiful face. I was having some special feeling for her but I didn't know whether it was LOVE or just an infatuation.

'Oh..Its 2.30 pm' I said on seeing my watch.

'Are you getting late for some work?' she asked.

'Yeah, I will catch you tomorrow at the same time' I said and left.

I reached the University Park where Mitali was waiting for me. We had met due to the cheeky and lucrative messages of the telecom service on mobile phone. She was not as beautiful as Vidisha was but she was sexy, had a modern look and was wearing a mini skirt.

'Hi, I am Mitali' she shook hands with me.

'I am sorry for last night. I was really busy' I told her.

'No problem' she gave a smile.

'Come on, let's sit for a coffee somewhere' I took her to Coffee Café Day.

Every guy in the park saw her seductive back and legs. I walked proudly beside this gorgeous looking girl. We sat in the café, her each movement redefined all the prototype style. She dragged her chair beside me and sat there. I started feeling her breath. She already gave me a hint that she was attracted towards me when we had long chats on the phone. But believing a big town girl could be very fatal. So I didn't reply to her that day.

We chatted for three hours, our past, our present and everything which we had experienced.

'So do you have any boy friend?' I asked with my fingers crossed.

'No, I had a recent break up with him' Mitali said.

'It's great. This is the kind of girl whom I was looking for, who will enjoy with me, seduce me and take me to bed without any commitment' I thought and I smiled as she gave her answer.

'I am single' I declared.

'But who asked?' Mitali said with a big smile.

Probably I had fired my gun at the right time.

'You look so beautiful and your sense of dressing is too good' I complemented her.

'Even you look good; at least better than my two previous boy friends' she said.

I didn't get what she wanted to say as I thought she was taking me as her next boy friend.

Finally we came out of the café and started to walk when rain interrupted and we both got drenched in the rain.

Mitali's hair got completely wet, her wet clothes stuck to her skin. A fine jet of water ran through her lips. I was getting attracted towards her.

I held her hand. She came close to me and it was happening on the first day of our meeting. And people said I had bad luck.

She kissed my cheeks thrice. I wanted to kiss her lips but managed to keep a distance as I thought I would do everything in the next meeting.

I escorted her to her hostel and decided to walk in the rain. An inevitable romance happened and I was the luckiest person. It was unbelievable how the last two days had been so happening for me.

With thoughts of Mitali; I was suddenly reminded of the last evening when I was with Vidisha. I was reminded of her treat, an unofficial date with a beautiful lady and today I romanced with another. I was romancing two beautiful women. I thought myself to be on the apogee of my career.

I could see the images of last night; I was intoxicated with feeling of love and lust.

She stood by my side, lifted her hair near the ear and said, 'PUT IT'

I smiled and took those ear rings and put them on to her ear. I felt the fragrance of a woman. She smiled while I was putting the rings on her ears.

Suddenly I was reminded of Vidisha, the entire scene appeared before me.

I took my hands out of my pocket, felt the drops of the rain on my palm.

'I LOVE YOU VIDISHA' I said to myself when suddenly a call interrupted my romantic mood.

It was a call from Vidisha.

'Hey, what's up? I was feeling bored so I called you up' Vidisha said.

'I am just outside my hostel, enjoying the rain' I said to her.

'Oh..I too like walking in the rain' Vidisha said.

'Come..We will roam across the lanes of the University' I tried to hook her.

'No, no…not now. I can't come out from my P.G now. Anyways

what's the matter? You are feeling quite romantic today' Vidisha smiled.

'Yeah…'I said.

'When my friend is so beautiful and when I have spent so much time with her then its destined to happen' I said and ran to take a shelter to protect my mobile phone from the rain.

'Ohhh…..'Vidisha gave blushes.

'I wish I could be with you now and could have enjoyed the rain with you' Vidisha gave me a lift.

'Don't worry; we will spend some time together in the rain.'

'OK then, just go to your room otherwise you will fall ill' she spoke like a motherly figure.

'Anything for you Ma'am' I went running inside my hostel.

She was about to end the call when I finally said, 'MISS YOU'

She didn't reply and rang off.

I went to the bathroom to wash the mud on my pants. I looked at the mirror; my cheeks had a red mark on it.

It was a kiss from Mitali that had left a mark on my face.

Suddenly I was reminded of Mitali, with my mind still preoccupied with thoughts of Vidisha.

I stood in front of my image and suddenly I started rubbing my cheeks. I washed it with water to remove the red stain.

I reached my room. Varun was playing some English song on his laptop.

'What's up man? Enjoying life with two beautiful ladies' Varun smiled at me.

'Yeah..But I don't know whom I like.'

'It's so easy, just ask your heart. Attraction is common at this age but true love is difficult to find.' Varun sounded like an elderly person. The guy gave huge *pravachans* without any prior experience.

I went to sleep. As I closed my eyes Vidisha came in my Dream in her beautiful pink dress. But there was no Mitali. At least my feelings were getting clearer and I was just behaving like any other teenager, getting attracted towards girls.

Every time I thought of Vidisha; every time I fell in love with her. Every time I saw her; my heart ran out of me to serve her. I didn't know how to react; I never felt the same for any girl. Love was casting its magic on me and changing me.

Love was not an easy path...

Days passed away ...I continued talking to Vidisha and Mitali.

'I am quite upset today' Vidisha said to me sipping his coffee.

'What happened?' I asked.

One of my childhood friends went on to propose to me. I didn't have that sort of feelings for him, but he insisted me to have such a relationship with him. I hate such friends who entertain such hopes. Can't a girl be a good friend?' she posed a question to me.

'Yeah, they can be.' I said hesitantly remembering 'Hum Tum's' Saif Ali Khan saying, 'Boys and girls can never be friends; love always comes in between'

'So can I ask one question?'

'What?' Vidisha asked.

'What's the difference between LOVE and ATTRACTION or INFATUATION?

'Love happens once, while attraction always changes. You might be attracted to someone on some day and it might change another day. But Love is pure; you know that you will be able to spend your life with that person, and that person's face will always keep you happy. That's the thing called Love. It's a divine feeling; you will know when you are in love.' Vidisha philosophized as if she had a Ph.D. degree on Love.

'I could feel it for you' I said to myself.

'But the feeling should be reciprocated, a single sided affair can be fatal' she continued.

My feelings was brought to reality as she talked of single sided talk.

I shook my head indicating that she was perfectly right.

I reached my room; Varun was sitting there playing his favorite car racing game.

'So, how are your two girl friends?' Varun asked.

'Both are good' I said smiling.

'But I guess one is attraction, the other is pure love.'

'So which one is which, tell me that' Varun said with huge anxiety in his mind and on his face.

'I love Vidisha. She is so simple and beautiful; she is the only girl with whom I can spend my entire life. I couldn't hide my emotions and I am doing wrong that I am roaming around with Mitali. If Vidisha comes to know that I am seeing one more girl then I won't cast a good impression on her.'

'So, you should tell Vidisha that you like her. This is her last year in college; she will leave college soon' Varun declared emergency.

'I can't, I don't know whether she likes me or not. I can't loose a precious friend like this. Someone proposed to her; the guy was her childhood friend and Vidisha hardly talks with him now. I don't want to speak my heart until I get some indication from her.'

'I think you are right; extract her feelings. Girls don't say it that easily' Varun said.

I took one of the seniors' bikes and started wandering on the roads of old Delhi and Chandni Chowk when suddenly I saw Vidisha.

'Day dreaming is bad' I said to myself when suddenly the girl waved to me; I just gave a smile to the girl and didn't stop.

'Armaan' she shouted.

I smiled, said, 'No to myself, as I thought it to be my day dreaming habits. I almost lost control on the bike and was about to fall.

I stopped the bike; the girl was indeed Vidisha.

'Hey, what are you doing here?' I stopped my bike close to her.

'Nothing; just came to meet my friend, but probably she is not in town today. So I am going back to the hostel now. But what about you?' she asked.

'I came to know that you will be found alone here so I came to take you back' I smiled as Vidisha looked suspiciously at me.

'Just kidding, I was wandering here and there as I was feeling bored in the hostel and suddenly I found you.'

I moved and made space for Vidisha to sit.

'Let's move' she said sitting decently on the bike. She held the seat with one hand and the projection on the back with the other hand. She didn't touch me at all. I was really getting impressed with her simple nature.

Suddenly rain started pouring as we crossed the Lal Quila.

I ran the bike under a shelter.

'Hey; let's move. Don't go under the shelter' Vidisha said which astonished me.

'Let's enjoy the rain together' she said winking his eyes.

'Why not' we came out of the shelter and speeded up the bike.

'I love rain' she said with her fingers demurely moving on my shoulders. For the first time she laid her hands on my shoulders. I could feel her soft hands on my shoulders.

We went for a long drive. We went to south Delhi, the Lotus Temple and finally to India Gate. A ride to India Gate on a bike on a rainy day and that too with the lady of your life was the best romance one could experience. With after each and every minute we were getting closer; her hands started to grip me.

We sat in park for an hour; her face was shining brilliantly with happiness.

After thirty five minutes of drive she demurely held me. I was falling for her. I wanted to announce my love but unfortunately we reached her P.G; the journey always seemed short. I left her and went back to the hostel when suddenly a message came on my mobile. I expected it to be from Vidisha as I could make it out that she was also falling in love.

But to my surprise she showed a desire to ride the bike. I gave space and allowed her to sit on the front. She was faltering in riding the bike showing that she was a new rider. I held her hand from behind, brought my face forward; we were very close to each other.

I couldn't believe my luck, after each passing second; my love for her was multiplying. Her simple thoughts, her smile had already clean bowled me. She took a sharp turn, our cheeks made a very soft contact as if saying 'Hi 'to each other. I couldn't believe on my luck. Still people said I had a bad luck. I held her hand to control the bike, an inevitable romance happened.

An accidental kiss happened; she smiled and suddenly stopped the bike. Vidya gave blushes as if it was her first kiss of life and didn't speak much about it.

'Now you drive and take me back' she said and felt the inevitable romance.

I realized for the first time how her happiness was making me happy.

I left her to her P.G and came back to hostel when suddenly a message came on my mobile. I expected it to be of Vidisha as I could make it out that she was also falling in love.

'Hey sweetheart; I am feeling quite romantic today. Let's go out somewhere and we will have fun. Missing you a lot.' Mitali's message came on my mobile.

I didn't know what to reply; I was in love with Vidisha and just wanted to hook Mitali. But Vidisha's simple nature taught me to be true at heart. And probably Vidisha changed my thought and I started believing in love and lifelong relationship.

'I am sorry dear; I am in love with someone else. You are just my friend and I am attracted towards you because you are good looking and I think we should part' I typed it frankly.

'You bastard, son of a bitch. What do you think of yourself? Boys want to have Mitali and you are going away and playing with my emotions. Go away from me; I will have thousands like you.' Mitali exploded through her message.

'Varun, you were right. Mitali never loved me; she was probably using me and was having fun. I was reminded of thousands of bucks which I had spent on her.'

'See, I told you; you will fall in love with only those who have a golden heart and all the rest are physical attractions.' Varun philosophized.

'You know what, you are a bitch' I typed my last message to Mitali and blocked her number on my mobile. I got satisfaction as I ended the game of lust.

Finally I realized my love, Vidisha. Farewell was near and I wanted to declare my love but still I couldn't speak up.

Finally the day of the farewell came. I made a card for Vidisha.

'Hey, tell her today. Don't think of the consequences, anyways she is leaving the college today. You might loose either way; why not be brave?' Varun said.

But Vidisha surprised everyone when she came wearing a pink saree for the farewell. She looked like a woman whom everyone would desire to marry. She wore the pink earrings which I gave her on her birthday. I was really happy as she considered my gift good enough to wear on a special occasion.

Fortunately I got a chance to dance with her. I gathered up enough courage to speak my heart.

The lecturers, professor and staffs of the college were sitting in front of us. I would have been screwed if I would have spoken a single word of proposal.

'These lecturers would screw me in their paper or probably flunk me. But if I couldn't speak today then the chance of proving my love would go in vain. I went near Vidisha, which caught the attention of everyone in the farewell party. The seniors gave a tough look as I was friendlier to Vidisha than my male seniors. She gave a small smile' I decided, ' I would speak today.'

'Who cares for a damn grade; anyways I will fuck it off. And these lecturers must have proposed someone in their life. Dr. Pandey looked seriously towards me; his expressions clearly indicated that my stupid act might be punished or maybe he would fail me in his paper. But if I don't say her today, I will lose her forever. I gave a cunning smile to my teachers.'

I went on my knees, ended the mind battle. Everyone looked at me, teachers stood from their place.

'I thought a lot about the definition of Love; I don't know how to define it when nobody in the universe has seen it but it has been felt by many. Everyone is in love with something, I thought a lot about this; my love will be one who is simple, with whom I can be comfortable and with whom I would not only love to live my entire life but also die.' I said to her with my eyes down on earth.

'So you got that person?' Vidisha asked.

If today I say I will make your life much happier, I might lie. I would like to grow old with you and prove my love, and if today I say that I waited for you since morning because I wanted to see you first in the farewell and would love to see you last when I die, then I won't say that I started loving you from today, but I would say that I would love you each and every day, each and every hour which we will spend together till I die. I finally said it to Vidisha, 'I LOVE YOU'.

Vidisha was surprised to hear that from me, she didn't expect it.

Even the doctors, lecturers were surprised to hear that. I knew I would be screwed up, but if she says YES then I will screw myself happily.

'See Vidisha, don't take me wrong. I wanted to say it before but I didn't because I wanted to say it on the last day so that you can understand that this is pure love and not just attraction and I would love you even when you are not in front of my eyes. Accept me as you are the only person whom I love in this lonely world, for me definition of love is you. I want to love you forever.'

Vidisha gave no answer, 'I don't know what to say. I am flattered.'

I kept on looking into her eyes and said, 'As a human being I have made many mistakes, may be I have flirted with some girls also but I promise you a great future and would never break your heart and would never repeat my mistakes.'

Vidisha didn't say anything and just left.

'Well done, let her decide now' Varun took my side.

I wish she says YES.

And I turned to go back when I saw all the lecturers standing behind me.

'Chill man, it's not a big issue. I would invite each of you in my marriage.'I thought of saying but their ferocious look stopped me from saying.

'Mr. Armaan. Can you explain the reason for your act?' Dr. Pandey, a man in his late fifties whose lecturers were as boring as he himself was. A man, who hardly showed his teeth in class, threw many students out of the class on being late or talking in class. I preferred to remain silent as I had no other option.

'Love' I thought and giggled.

'Do you come to College for such things and what were you doing today?'one of the lecturers prompted from behind.

'Common man, didn't you see I just proposed her. I love her. And yeah many come to college for such things.' I thought of saying.

I wish I could tell him that I saw his daughter kissing a guy in front of the entire college. And the same man was talking of the discipline which he couldn't impose on his own daughter. It was very difficult to make him understand that things have changed. Now India is no more backward, and the mentality of the people has also changed. Old generation people can never understand the Y generation.

'Such things happen in big cities'Varun prompted from behind.

I couldn't resist my laugh which irritated the teachers standing in front of me.

'You are gone; I will see that you are suspended this year. And I will screw you in my paper.'They said loudly and left.

'Who cares, anyways I am going to get screwed in your paper.'I blinked my eyes to Varun, gave a smile and proceeded towards the hostel.

'She will say YES, don't worry other wise she would have directly told you a big NO' Varun said. Girls take time in taking a decision.

We went to our room. We were watching a tennis match when suddenly a message peep was heard in the silent T.V room.

Roger Federer launched a perfect ace against his rival Nadal.

I opened my inbox anxiously expecting a YES from Vidisha. I left the T.V room, Varun followed me.

I opened her message, 'You flirt, you flirted with Mitali, and she is my roommate's sister. You took her for dates, enjoyed the monsoon with her; kissed her. And you left her and I can't believe that the same person is talking about commitment and love.'

I stood dejectedly, Varun peeped into the message.

'Hey, write her that she was a bitch. She already had two break ups and you were just attracted to her' Varun said loudly.

I wrote to Vidisha but it was difficult to persuade her and I didn't want to present Mitali's bad image to Vidisha and her sister coz I was equally guilty.

'I didn't expect this from you; I really thought of you after you declared your love but I can't go with such a person who used a girl and left her. I am leaving Delhi tomorrow forever. B'bye............'

her last message looked as if she won't contact me after this.

The world came crashing down; tears rolled down my cheeks. Varun saw this and gave solace to me.

'So no more boring stuff of love now, nothing is enjoyable. Let's party' Varun said trying to change the atmosphere.

I looked at him; tried to hide all my sorrows and said, 'Let's party'

We went to the BLUES and started boozing.

We drank till 4 in the morning but I didn't utter a single word. I wanted to gulp all the miseries of my life with the wine. We reached back to the hostel.

The next day in college was very quiet for me with no Vids(Vidisha) around. Varun became closer to me and we became inseparable friends in a very short time. My mood of romance suddenly changed to that of tragedy.

I said sorry to all my professors for my misbehavior.

One day I got a call from an anonymous number. I thought it to be from Vidisha.

I took the call with excitement.

'Hello' the voice didn't sound like Vidisha's.

'This is Varun's mother; just tell Varun that his father is serious and has been admitted to the hospital. And tell him to come at the CURE hospital in Daryaganj' the voice almost broke.

Varun was playing his favorite tune on the guitar. I didn't know how to break such a bad news to him.

I went to him and said at one go, 'Your mother called me up and informed that your father is serious. Let's go to the hospital'.

Varun stopped playing the guitar and his fingers got stuck in between the wires and started bleeding profusely. The tension could easily be made out from his face.

I bandaged his hand and we went to the hospital.

The scene was pathetic there; Varun's dad died of to cancer. His mother kept on crying.

But Varun was a brave man. He went to his mother; gave her solace. He knew that he was the only person on this earth who could make his mother bear this shock.

I decided to leave the place as I was getting sentimental too. I went outside the hospital; I started crying. I felt Varun's pain and cried over my personal losses too.

I went back to the hostel after informing Varun about it.

Varun decided to stay with his mother and left the hostel. He sometimes visited the hostel to meet me and sometimes slept for a night in my room. He liked living in the hostel but his responsibilities did not allow him to enjoy the same thing.

A year passed by, memories of Vidisha still haunted me.

We somehow managed to clear the IIT entrance and were reaching to go to IIT Bombay for the Master's degree.

'I will leave my mom at my brother's place in Allahabad and then will come to Bombay' Varun said to me.

Soon our college days got over and we were about to leave Delhi.

I reached New Delhi railway station to board my train.

I got on to the Rajdhani Express; suddenly I smelt the fragrance of Vidisha. I could feel her presence around me. I kept my belongings on my seat and came out of the train in the hope of seeing Vidisha at the station. I looked here and there, wandered on the platform.

I dejectedly came back to my berth as I didn't find her. I could still feel her.

I got on tothe upper berth; suddenly I recognized a voice.

'100 rupees' the female voice said to the coolie.

I came down instantaneously; the girl turned towards me.

'Vidisha...'I said.

'Armaan..' she said.

'How come you are here? 'I asked her.

'I am going to Surat, I work there' she sounded professional.

She took her seat; luckily she was sitting in font of me.

'We were destined to meet.' I said to her.

'It's just a fourteen hour journey' she said.

'No, it's the fourteen hours of my life.'

'So you still entertain hopes of getting me?' she asked a simple question.

'You are the only girl whom I love; this is what I know.'

'So Mr. Flirty how is your life going on? There must be a lot of girls in your life' she asked making a huge mockery of my true love.

'I am joining IIT Bombay and there is no girl in my life.' I replied smartly.

'Good for you' she said.

'But I might not join it if...' I paused.

'If..' she repeated it.

'If we run away from our home today, I will do any job. I will always love you and we will get married one day. If our family accepts us then we will come back otherwise we will make our own small world full of love. What do you say? Let's run away, the setting is perfect for it.' I blinked at her.

'Are you nuts? Come back to reality..' She said.

She didn't talk much and made me feel guilty. She went to her berth and slept as if she care didn't for me.

I kept on observing her; she was the most beautiful woman I had ever seen in my life and I loved her from the bottom of my heart.

She was wearing the same pink earrings which I had given her. I didn't know why but I guessed it was just accidental or may be she liked me.

A woman's heart is the most difficult thing to read.

'I am SORRY, please don't go away like this' I wrote on a blank sheet of paper and kept it near Vidisha.

I don't know how I slept observing her beautiful face as I had decided not to sleep and to spend the entire night observing her.

I woke up to find the berth in front of me empty. She had left without even saying 'Bye'.I found my letter kept there, she probably didn't even open it. I was really heart broken; a bit angry too.

I reached IIT Bombay; Varun came after a few days and we joined the classes in this great institution of India.

Varun and I were again made room mates. We went to booze on the eve of Varun's birthday, our favorite pastime.

We made some new friends; Rajeev was one of them; though a junior but a very decent and a nice chap.

'Hi.Rajeev' a seducing voice interrupted us as we were drinking as usual, on a Friday, which we hade made our boozing day.

'Hi, Tanya.' Rajeev said.

Tanya was one of the beautiful girls in IIT and was Rajeev's classmate.

There is a very famous adage invented by none other than our own brainstorming IITians. In IIT there are two genders; one is male and the other is non male. There is no such divine beauty called female in IIT but Tanya was one of the few exceptions.

Rajeev introduced Tanya to us. The girl was quite frank and open minded.

She took out her cigarette and started smoking.

'Why don't you join us?' Varun said.

She sat with us and from a group of three people we became a gang of four, only one short of the famous five.

'She seems to be a modern and an advanced girl' I murmured to Rajeev.

'Yeah' Rajeev said.

I got a place in the IIT cricket team. Varun, Rajeev and Tanya came to see all my matches. In a short span of time we became good friends.

One day Tanya called me up.

'Hi…' she said.

'Hello..Wass up baby?' I asked.

'Nothing much, let's go out to have some food' she said.

'OK, are others coming?' I asked locking my room.

'No, just you and me' she said.

'Anything special today?' I inquired.

'Nothing special. Hey, I will catch you at the main gate after fifteen minutes. Be there on time; I will tell you everything' she kept the phone down.

'Hey, where are you going?' Varun asked me.

I am going to dine with Tanya. She called me up just a few minutes back.

'Ohh....so another girl in your life' Varun said.

Naa...Just a friend and nothing more. I was not able to make up my mind whether I could settle down with Tanya because I was still haunted by thoughts of Vidisha.

'Think on this; she seems to be a nice girl. I guess she is better than Mitali' Varun shouted from behind making me realize how I had played with girls in the past.

I stopped. But not better than Vids; there can be noone like her.' I gave really a flat and solid answer proving myself to be true.

'Common man, forget her. She didn't even bother to contact you and it has been more than a year that she broke up with you. It's time to forget her now and look at the future.' Varun said.

Still, love happens once. And I knew I loved her truly and we will meet one day. I remembered SRK in K_2H_2 that love happens only once.

Varun was in no mood to catch these sentimental dialogues,' 'Just remember one thing, you learn from your past. When someone has left you, just move on. A new world waits for you. Just take a plunge in it. He proved that even SRK fell twice in love in K_2H_2.

I reached the main gate. For the first time I kept on thinking of Varun's word.

I took Tanya to Pizza Hut. For the first time, I found her beautiful.

We took a stroll near Powai Lake after having some pizzas. I kept on observing her small activities, her smile and her body movements. I had never felt the same way for Tanya as I was feeling today. I was looking at her with the same emotions that I had had for Vidisha. Probably I found solace in her.

She held my hand while she tried to sit on the small rock near the shore of the lake. Time passed away and in a year Tanya became close to me but she knew that I didn't love her.

'Common let's move, we are getting late. Ashish Ranjan, the CEO of the blockbuster company MYgames the baron would arrive anytime' Varun told me as we moved to the Lecture theatre for the E Summit organized by the Entrepreneurship cell.

Finally the baron came and was felicitated.

Vinod, the student's head of the E Summit started the proceedings.

'All big businesses were small companies once; all small companies were start once. The big skyscraper building offices were once confined to a single room office, a million dollar company was not even worth thousand once. Some people sitting in a small gloomy room thought something innovative and went ahead and from a small group of individuals became a unit of thousands and became the biggest company. It happened just because a few people sitting in that room or roaming around just like us thought something out of the box; implemented it with the team, became entrepreneurs and showed many people how to run a business and earn fame and money. This is the power of entrepreneurship', Vinod was stopped by the loud round of applause by the audience. Even the business barons sitting there appreciated the speech of this whiz kid.

We were also impressed by the mindboggling speech which talked of the ground realities and which became the future later.

'I never thought this way' Varun said.

'I thought studying and then doing some job was only beneficial' Rajeev said.

I remained silent as I was more interested in watching the business barons sitting at the dais of the auditorium. I also wanted to become one of those, wearing etiquette attires, travelling in a chartered flight, Mercedes Benz, dining in five star hotels, having my own cruise and lots of money.

'I just wanted to become rich and wear black suits like them' I said looking at the industrialists.

Vinod continued, 'But one thing is for sure; it's not meant for only high class people; a start up can even be run by mediocre people. If you think you have a unique idea and it can change the course of the nation, affect many lives, bring wealth and believe me there is no other better job and satisfaction than to start your own company.'

The center stage was occupied by a few entrepreneurs who had come to showcase their own innovative businesses and a few big barons who were the guests of honor.

It made me remember of my Punjabi neighbors, who always flaunted their wealth which they made by opening a chain of women's cloth shop. They started with a very small shop and now they were earning a lot. Anyways Punjabis usually prefer business over a job; the thought cleared soon as there is a famous saying among Punjabis.'Punjabis get married when they own a business, a working class Punjabi finds difficult to find a bridegroom.'

Finally Ashish was welcomed on to the center stage, he gave a brief lecture on his company, a company that started off as a gaming zone in the city market and went on to become a big company in a year.

Who would have thought Indians would be so fascinated by egames? But the success of the company tells the story.

'Success is in thinking differently and uniquely' Ashish finally left the dais.

We started moving towards our hostel. We got attracted towards the entrepreneurship idea.

A year passed, we became very good friends. Tanya started liking me and started spending more time with me but I didn't like her that way; she was just a friend to me. I tried to contact Vidisha through our common friends but couldn't manage to get her personal number; dejectedly, I tried to find solace in Tanya and she thought it was love. I too found peace while talking to her; though she could never replace Vidisha.

Exuberance of Youth…

We were becoming spendthrifts like any other youth who wanted to have fun and an adventurous life. After a year of fun we started running short of money. We even took loans from our friends and so we did what most people do to earn money without realizing its consequences. We came in contact with Vinod, an entrepreneur by choice who was running an Online Job portal and had launched an official website too. Abhisek, a skilled I.T professional and one of our friends made a website for him. He started his small business with his friends and was looking for some more people to work with him. We started up our own venture, capitalized on Vinod's idea and copied his business model.

'Cheers' I clinked my glass of wine with Varun and Rajeev.

'Yeah..' Everyone complemented each other.

We didn't know the long term plan of this business which he had started. We only knew it was a source of backup money.

We were jubilant to find our first client. He needed a good counseling and a proper tuning for the jobs available in the market.

We googled all the sectors in the market for his queries and we received our first cheque of five thousand rupees; a small amount but a good pocket money for three people.

We celebrated our efforts and went to our favorite cheap road side bar. We found Vinod there.

'So, how are you?' I asked him and appreciated his speech on Entrepreneurship which he had given few days back.

'Thanks. I heard you have started your business too' Vinod asked us.

'Yeah..' Varun said proudly.

'That's really good' Vinod joined us.

We ordered some Vodka shots and in just a few minutes we gulped it down and felt intoxicated.

'But our business still doesn't sound unique' Vinod said sipping his Romanov.

'Who cares, as long as we are getting good clients and filling our pockets? Who cares for the uniqueness' I said.

'Yeah, rightly said.'Varun complemented me.

'But what about the future, a time will come when your business will get exhausted and you will get no clients. You have to position ourselves against the existing competitors.You need to update new features on your website, think something innovative which existing competitors don't offer in the market. I guess we should approach some investors, angel investors who will fund us and we can become a bigger name in the market. Don't take it lightly; this is the best thing one can do in one's life....One's own company' Vinod didn't sound alcoholic and behaved like a sober and an intelligent guy.

He was quite serious about his business and wanted to mould it according to his own wishes.

'But let's enjoy our first success, we will do this later' Varun ordered one more bottle of beer.

I took one drag of cigarette from Vinod, I tasted it after a year and I could feel the thirst in my throat for more. I got a packet of cigarettes and started smoking again.

Vinod joined hands with us; we merged our business model and started working together.

We left the Bar and reached our room. We converted our room into a small business office, and named it Corporate Office of JOBS MADE EASY and we named the company as JOBS MADE EASY as it was started by people living in the same wing, wanting their lives to be easy.

I emptied my room and we placed three computers there; placed a board where we recorded all the transactions and a few self motivating posters. For the next few days we were busy in mining all the data of different companies, the kind of jobs they offer, their packages and other minute details.

We became quite busy, attending classes in the morning and then working for our own company at night.

But every day one of us managed some time and browsed through all the information. In three months we had a good number of records, data of different company and archive files. We were getting clients but not on a regular basis, so we contacted Vinod for some help as he was the founder of this company. But he was travelling a lot due to his academic projects. So we really had to fix up a meeting before we could meet him.

'Hey man. What's up?' Varun exchanged a smile with the suave guy; Vinod.

'I am fine, just getting along with my classes. And how are you and how is the company doing? I am sorry I am not able to take out time for it but I will be back very soon.' Vinod said.

'This is why we have come to meet you; actually we are getting very few clients these days' Varun said as I looked towards Vinod for an answer.

'It's just because we are a small company; we don't have a marketing strategy and as I already told you we need to bring out some innovative products too.'Vinod replied.

'So what do we need to do?' I asked him frankly.

'Well then; let's sit tonight and decide what exactly we need to do' Vinod was about to close his door when we moved out.

'Are you nuts? Why we are including him in our team? It's just a part time business and now we will have to share the money among four people.' I argued with Varun lighting my cigarette.

'You have again started smoking' Varun said.

'Don't worry man; I take only two-three in a day.'

We reached our room cum office when suddenly my phone rang.

'Hey swetuuu.........Can we go for a movie tonight?' Tanya was on the line.

'How many times have I told you not to call me by that name, it's really irritating. I can't go anywhere today; actually we have to work for our company. So I am really busy; maybe we can go next weekend.' I said, as Varun switched on the three computers.

'It's OK' Tanya sounded humble.

'I am sorry but not today' I too replied humbly.

'Miss you Jaanuuuu...' she made a sound of a kiss on the phone.

I was getting attracted to Tanya but the thought of Vidisha in my mind always kept me away from Tanya.

'I think this girl is falling for you' Varun said risibly.

'But I like Vidisha; it's again getting too complex for me.'

'It's a love triangle then' Varun smiled.

'A triangle in which no sides meet; it's just three intersecting lines or probably three different planes' I said.

We exchanged smiles when Vinod and Rajeev joined us.

Vinod opened the company's website,'www.jobsmadeeasy.com'

We appreciated the website.

'See we need to have a better website and some new features should be added on this page. It looks very dull and we have to keep updating it regularly' Vinod started browsing for templates.

'I think we need to move out of this room' Vinod said. The statement was like a fast running jet which none could comprehend.

'We didn't get you' Rajeev murmured.

'I mean we need to move out of this room and have a proper office. I have a few innovative ideas which will certainly change the fate of the company. But first we need to get some investors who will put their money in our business. We need some angel investors' Vinod announced proudly.

'Angel investors. What's that?' Rajeev's query was to the point.

'An angel investor or angel is an affluent individual who provides capital for a business start up, usually in exchange for convertible debt or ownership equity. A small but increasing number of angel investors organize themselves into angel groups or angel networks to share research and pool their investment capital. Angels typically invest their own funds, unlike venture capitalists, who manage the pooled money of others in a professionally-managed fund' Vinod showed his intelligence.

'And I guess if we get good sponsors then we will certainly make money from the Indian Market' Varun appreciated the idea.

One day we finally got another client. We decided again to party. After having shots of Vodka we decided to move back.

'Wait, I will bring some cigarettes.' I frantically searched my pocket.

'Take my bike, bring it form Hiranandani' Vinod handed over the keys to me.

'But be alert; if you are caught driving in an inebriated state; you will be screwed' Varun made me realize that it's a crime.

But when you are young, you think laws are meant to be broken without thinking of the consequences. Everything is taken for granted.

I took the bike and was about to reach Hiranadani when I saw a mobile police jeep coming towards me. I parked the bike and decided to walk to the shop; I wanted to avoid any hiccups.

It was very dark, with clouds hovering in the sky. It looked as if it would rain anytime. The lightening and the thunder made the night look even worse; the place was deserted.

I took out a cigarette and started smoking; with my head spinning due to excess Vodka shots, I tried to bring back myself to the dusty and gloomy road. I looked towards the street light when I realized that I was in the middle of the road.

I was about to reach the footpath when a speeding car honking continuously came rushing towards me.

I was not able to walk properly and tried to control myself. Suddenly that speeding car almost ran me over when I shouted from the back in an inebriated state.

'You bloody, can't you see people walking around?' I shouted at the car but it didn't have any impact on the driver and it continued to move in the same fashion.

I threw the bottle of wine lying in the corner of the ground, with a compelling force. It hit the car on the back.

'Now just go' I shouted again and laughed.

The speeding car lost its balance and it went on to hit a big tree, the engine caught fire.

'You deserve this' I laughed as the car toppled over.

I turned back; suddenly the window of the car crashed and a female was thrown out of it.

She was bleeding profusely. I ran towards her to help her. As I went near her; there was a clash of lightning; I saw the face of that female for the first time.

I was brought back to my senses.

'Vidisha.........you...............' I held her head in my hand as it thundered and rain started pouring down from the dark sky.

Vidisha got a glimpse of me. Blood started to flow profusely from the back of her head.

Tear started rolling down my cheeks, my hands and legs trembled. There was not a single person on the road, I ran towards the road as I saw a car racing down the street. I rushed towards it for help.

'Hey, Stop.....Stop Please....'I cried at the top of my voice, the car didn't stop. I saw Vidisha making some movement. I ran towards her.

This is Armaan, remember. I love you and I am sorry for what I did, you will be absolutely fine. I will take you to the hospital. Vidisha saw me and finally closed her eyes and fainted.

'Vids........Someone please help me. Is there no one?' I shouted at the top of my voice which soon died off in the empty road.

I rushed towards my bike; held Vidisha in my arms and took her to a private hospital. The feeling of guilt filled my mind.

Finally I admitted her to a hospital, looking at her critical condition she was directly taken into the I.C.U. I was feeling guilty as if I had murdered someone.

I called Varun for help; he came rushing to the hospital. I narrated to him the entire story of what had happened.

With each word I spoke, I felt more guilty and stricken with remorse. Tears started rolling down as Varun tried to give some solace to me.

'Don't feel this way; what you did was wrong and you got punishment from God by hurting your own love. Now just help her; she needs somebody with her and when she recuperates then just express your feeling of guilt, she will understand you and your feeling this time' Varun said and left.

I sat in the hospital for the entire night; police came in to inquire about the accident. But we could not get the information about Vidisha's family.

I sat outside the I.C.U praying for her good health when I started visualizing Vidisha, and I dozed off.

I was reminded of that rainy day when we had enjoyed the rain on the bike in Delhi; she was looking absolutely stunning in her simple dress that day and today on a bloody rainy night; I hurted her.

Blood started flowing profusely, she looked at me and I ran across the road to get some help. My small sleep was broken by such chain of thoughts.

I had begun to sweat; dejectedly I went near the I.C.U where she was getting operated.

'I am sorry dear' I said in my mind as I saw the doctor operating on her skull. I looked towards the sky praying to the heavenly powers dwelling there to take her out of this pain.

'If today I say I will make your life much happier, I might lie. I would like to grow old with you and prove my love and if today I say that I waited for you since morning because I wanted to see you first in farewell and would love to see you last when I die then I won't say that I started loving you from today but I would say that I would love you each and every day, each and every hour which we will spent together till I die. I finally said it to Vidisha, 'I LOVE YOU' I still remember the proposal lines which I had spoken to Vidisha on the eve of their farewell. The words were echoing in my ear. I repeated the lines again with tears in my eyes and a shrunken voice.

After several hours of examination and operation the doctors came out of the I.C.U. I ran towards them to inquire about Vidisha's condition.

'Well, she will be kept on ventilators for a few more hours until her system re adjusts and supports her. Blood has collected in her head due to her head hitting the road hard; she is still in a critical condition. She is in COMA' the doctor directed me to the fees counter. I was stunned after hearing the word coma and all because of my bloody deed.

'Coma….' The word echoed in my mind. I blamed myself for this disaster in her life.

The nurse directed me to the cash counter. The bill was too high for a student like me to pay. We went to the director and the chairman of the hospital to request for a fees waiver. The chairman was a nice chap and agreed to operate Vidisha free of cost; probably he showed generosity to the YOUTH whom he addressed as the FUTURE OF THE NATION.

We heaved a huge sigh of relief as the bill had mounted quite high.

For the next few days; we started contacting the investors and the angel investors and got responses from them.

'Hey; Army. I guess we will have a big deal tomorrow. The investors have called us for a presentation of our idea, so we need to work out our presentation' Vinod said.

'It's great; we will definitely have one investor tomorrow. I promise you, the presentation and our show will be awesome.' Varun got charged up as we had been waiting for just this opportunity.

'Yeah, we will pull it off tomorrow but I will not be able to sit now with you all and discuss about the presentation as I have to go to the hospital now. Vidisha is still in a critical condition' I said and was about to move when Rajeev interrupted me.

'OK, but make sure that you come tomorrow. The entire team should go to their office' Rajeev said as I went out lighting my cigarette.

'I don't know what this chap will do; he is hardly spending time with us and talking business. His love affair has taken him away from us' Vinod said.

'Don't worry, he will come back. I know him very well. He is really upset these days because of Vidisha's accident' Varun tried to defend me.

'Anyways let's hope that she recuperates soon and Armaan spends more time on the business,' Vinod said as all of us sat together discussing the contents of the presentation.

I reached the hospital; the scene was pathetic there; filled with wails and pain of many people. I directly went to Vidisha's cabin room where she was going to get operated. The nurses were cutting her hair.

'Hey; why are you doing this?' I asked them.

'Her cut on the skull is not visible clearly so we need to cut her hair, so that we can operate on her skull' the nurse started cutting those silky hairs.

I am so sorry, Vids. It's because of me that you are suffering. I cursed myself and sat beside her. The nurses made her bald; the scars on her face, the bald head and a long cut on her head changed her look completely. Now the heavenly beauty looked like a patient fighting for her life.

The nurses left after cutting her hair and granted me fifteen minutes to sit in the cabin.

I went near her; she looked blankly at my face. Those beautiful eyes looked expression less, her eyes were moist. I looked into her eyes with a feeling of guilt gripping my mind.

I put my lips close to her ears and blurted out my emotions knowing that she would not be hearing me.

'I am so sorry. Please forgive me. I love you.' I could utter only these three sentences as my voice chocked due to tears in my eyes. I went outside and sat in front of her room.

I fell asleep and was woken up by the cleaning staff of the hospital.

'Oh…Fuck..It's 10 am and I didn't go back to the hostel last night. I was reminded of the presentation which was scheduled at 10 am. I took out my mobile, found 15 missed calls from Varun. I called him back but there was no response. I hurriedly left the hospital and went to the hostel to find our office cum room closed. Probably the trio had left for the presentation and I was late.

I came back to the hospital; while going to the hospital I found a girl in rags pulling my jeans at the red light stop.

'Bhaiya..yeh flowers le lo apne doston ke liye; apne pyar ke liye'

'Brother..Take these roses for your friends and your love' the innocent girl looked at me.

The ragged condition of the girl aroused sympathy in my mind and I took those flowers. The girl ran to her mom, who was sitting at the red light, with a big smile, when I handed her the money. I had never thought myself to be so emotional.

I took those red roses and kept them beside Vidisha, they were her favorite red roses, but she was not there to appreciate them.

I held her palm in mine when suddenly her fingers made some movements and for the first time; she made eye contact with me. I looked into her eyes and she looked into mine.

'Why do you love me so much?' she asked. I shouted for the doctors as they came rushing towards the room.

I looked into her eyes, kissed her hand when suddenly the doctor came from behind.

'Sir, she is making movements, she spoke' I shouted on top of my voice.

'What are you doing? Why are you pressing her hand? Can't you see she is in a coma? Now just go and leave her. We have to operate on her.' the doctor brought me back from my dreams.

After six hours of operation, the doctor came out.

'How is her condition Sir? Is she recuperating? Will she come out of the coma?' I fired all possible questions at one go.

'She is out of danger now and she is out of coma too. But it will take a week more for her to recuperate as she is quite weak now. She is making only hand movements.' I heaved a huge sigh of relief as the doctor broke the good news.

'But she is sleeping now; you can see her tomorrow' the doctor said and left.

I went back to the hostel and reached back to find my business colleagues celebrating.

'What happened?' I asked them.

'Our business plan got selected among ten other plans and now there is only one interview next week and then we will be a big company' Vinod proudly announced the good result.

'Let's go out and party' Rajeev said.

'Yeah why not' Varun and I agreed to the idea.

'Hey Armaan; I need to say one thing to you' Varun said to me.

'I also want to tell you something.'

'You know what, Vidisha is recuperating fast and she is out of the coma. Isn't it great news?' I didn't allow Varun to say what he wanted to say.

'Good' Varun gave a cold response.

'What happened? You don't look in good spirits.'

'I wanted to say that you are not able to give your time to us and our business. You know the investor asked us today where is the fourth person and we gave some ludicrous excuses but this is not at all professional behavior. You didn't even turn up last night for discussing the presentation. I know she needs you but your professional career also needs you and here is a team of three people who equally needs you. So you should manage your time properly.' Varun said.

'I know; I am not able to give enough time to my professional life and I am maintaining a distance from you all but just give me one more week. In that time she will recuperate and I promise I will work even harder.'

'But you should try to give some time to the business also. Just come for the meetings, come and sit in the office and just observe what all things are happening in our start up. I think you should manage that much time in your busy life' Varun's word pinched me but I knew that I was wrong so I didn't continue the insatiable debate.

'I will be there in the meeting next week. I promise you and after that I will be there forever.'

First we went to the hospital to see Vidisha. Varun couldn't even identify Vidisha because of the cuts and her bald head. I could make out from his face that he was feeling pity for the girl.

We continued to the bar after visiting the hospital; no one talked and we sat silently in the bar without even ordering any drink.

'Hey let's just celebrate our first effort' I tried to cheer them up.

Everyone gave a cold response and after having only one peg we decided to check out. Probably everyone was upset after seeing Vidisha.

I came back to the hospital next morning; bought roses from that same ragged girl. I entered the ward room; the nurse was giving feeding food to her.

I went and sat beside her, took the jar of liquid food from the nurse and started feeding Vidisha.

Vidisha kept on looking into my eyes; I smiled and placed the red rose in her hand. She kept it beside her and held my hands.

I smiled back; probably she was expressing thanks through her eyes for doing so much for her. She blinked both her eyes. She didn't know that I was her culprit.

I went down on my knees; held my ear and said,' I am sorry dear'

She gave a small smile; her beautiful hands were pierced with tubes. I was happy to see her coming back to life.

I took her in my arms and placed her on a wheel chair and brought her out of that claustrophobic room. She saw the sun's light and felt the fresh air after five days. I took her to the garden, placed a white rose over her ear. Tears came rolling down as I was reminded of the day when I presented the earrings to this beautiful divine girl. I turned away to hide my tears and took her back to her ward room. The doctor told me to leave her alone and allow her to sleep; she held my hands expressed a desire through her eyes to sit with her as she was feeling afraid. I transmitted confidence through my eyes; raised her from the wheel chair and placed her on the bed. I drew the linen over her and held her hand. She felt asleep in a few minutes and I came back to the hostel.

A week later...

Varun, Vinod and Rajeev were working hard for the company. I was not able to give time to them and it was creating a distance between us but I had no choice.

'Hey sit. You came at the right time. We are finally giving a brief presentation of our business and our own profile. Join us' Varun said as he opened the file on his laptop.

We sat together and discussed the things we needed to address to our investors but my mind was preoccupied with thoughts of Vidisha.

'Armaan, be ready tomorrow for the presentation; we will leave by 10 am.' I was brought back from the hospital scene to the proceedings in the room by Varun, as I was present only physically but mentally was absent.

I nodded like an obedient student and went to sleep with my mind still occupied with thoughts of Vidisha.

I reached the hospital at 6 am in the morning; made a point to buy roses from that ragged girl. The girl smiled as she saw me, folded the money in her hand; gave me blessing and ran towards her mother. She looked very innocent even in her shabby and ragged clothes.

I straightway went into Vids' room, she was sleeping. As I sat there, I found a paper floating in the air. It caught my attention as something was written on it.

I caught the paper. Something was scribbled on it; I identified the handwriting as that of Vid's and started reading it.

Another window to my dreams opened

Pure and eternal showers of blessings poured in

The feeling in me was divine

As now my fructification was going to fructify

Then a creation now a creator

I dreamt of fabricating a dream world for my creation.

Apprehensive tides pervaded my sea of thoughts

As the bud in me blossoms into a flower on the crest of my perturbed thoughts hovered my consternation

Then pearls of hope sparkled on the bosom of my trepidation

As someone whispered "you my creator I plead thee do not fear as your fear uneasiness agonizes me.

I am being nurtured within you.

Your dreams have taught me to dream

As you see beyond that open window from where pure and eternal showers of blessings pour upon me.

Where time flies like a breeze

Wait till my accouchement; don't let your heart freeze"

Startled I was by the whisper

I gazed around myself

Then realized it was creation whispering.

Suddenly I felt a pain.

Blood gushed down my veins

Suddenly I heard the whisper again…

I couldn't believe that Vidisha was such a good writer; I turned the page.

'I am sorry; I took you in a wrong way. You are a very good human being.' I read the writing on the back of the paper.

'I am missing you, where are you right now? I have not slept the entire night and was waiting for you.' I looked at that innocent face of Vidisha. 'Thank you for everything...........'

I took the pen out from my pocket.

'Anything for you Ma'am' I wrote and kept the paper near her when suddenly she woke up. She saw me and turned her sight away from me.

I understood; she was angry and was probably asking why I was late.

'I gave her the roses. Sorry dear......' I looked into her eyes.

She behaved like any other girl and turned away.

I took her hand in mine and kissed it.

She smiled and said, 'Why do you love me so much?'

I was hearing her voice after two years.

I smiled and said, 'I can't help dear. I love you just because you make my soul feel pure and natural when I am with you'

She blushed and didn't utter any more sentences as the doctor had advised her not to speak much. I took the paper and started writing.

'I am sorry; you are suffering because of my foolish act; I never thought in my wildest dreams that it can be you in that car.' I wrote and showed it to her.

'It seems we were destined to meet this way; we met in train for 14 hours and now everything was planned by the God.' She wrote back.

"DESTINY DESIRES EVERYTHING"

'But I can't see you in such agony. I wish I could take away your pain' I wrote again.

'Don't worry; I will be fine very soon. We had to meet this way only. Whatever happened is past and I guarantee our future will be very great. Great buddies meet like this to create history' she passed the paper to me.

My watch said 9 am and I got ready to leave the hospital, when she held my hands.

'Don't go. The hospital is a very boring place and I miss you' she whispered.

'Hey, I need to go. I have an important meeting now.'

She behaved like a normal girl, turned away from me and said in a cold manner, 'Bye then.'

'Please understand me; I need to go' I insisted.

'Can you take me out for a few minutes? I want to see the sun. Enjoy like before' she interrupted. I submitted myself to the divine beauty.

'She is here because of me but they also need me. She can't manage here without me until her family comes here, she has no one here. But Varun, Vinod and Rajeev are together; only I am missing and they can fill in my place' my spirit started saying to me and I decided not to go. I was caught up in a trade off of duty and heart, in which eventually, the heart won.

I took her to the garden in a wheel chair. She felt delighted on seeing the sun.

'You can leave if you want' she said calmly.

'No, it's OK, my friends will manage without me' I said.

'I am working in Surat; just came here for an official deal. I learnt driving last month only, and was trying my hand when the accident happened' she said.

It happened because of me.

'I don't think so; I already told you that it was destined to happen this way. But I got to see a new face of yours, especially after whatever I learned from my friend about you and your flirty nature. But you seem to be sensitive and a caring guy. Finally I am impressed' she said smilingly. I saw that smiling face after so many days.

'I still like you and believe me this love will never die.'

'I need some time' she said frankly.

Finally the romance was back in the air; it seemed like love needed no season to blossom; it happens spontaneously. My feelings for her were becoming more pronounced.

'I will always love you' I murmured.

Finally I took her back to her room and placed her on her bed to rest.

'I will miss you, do come early tomorrow' Vidisha said as I was about to move.

I gave a smile and came out of the hospital. I punched the air, skipped down few staircases. She was also feeling the intoxicating love. I knew she had started loving me all over again. I reached the room where Varun had been waiting for me endlessly.

'Hey, you know what...Vidisha misses me too' I said with a big smile on my face.

Varun gave no response.

'Fuck off......The investors turned off and we are not getting a single penny from them. We have to close our business; it was just a part time business.' Varun said angrily and moved out of the room and was making me feel guilty.

I followed him.

'I am so sorry; I couldn't come today but she needed me too.'

'And what about us?' Vinod said.

'From today; just be happy with her. In any case we are going to close this part time business. You know the investor again inquired about you; he wondered how a member could be so irresponsible.' We didn't have any answer. And we kept quiet and they thought that we are not serious about this business' Varun entered into his gloomy room.

'I am so sorry; we can try some other investor.' I said.

Varun slammed the door hard on my face, making me feel guilty.

I entered in that gloomy room, Vinod was also sitting there when suddenly someone pushed me hard. The force almost made me fall down and then the figure started yelling at me. I turned to see the person; it was my best buddy; Varun.

'You know we are also having classes and many more commitments in our personal life but we always thought that we would open this company by working hard and managing time. All our efforts have been wasted just because of you and I think I cannot work anymore with you' Vinod said and left the room announcing that he was no more with us.

'Chill man, anyways this business was just a small source of income to us and nothing more' I sounded much friendly to Varun, after Vinod left.

'You know I thought you were more responsible. You always wanted to be a business man and look at your approach. I can't believe you could change this way' Varun kept on reproaching me.

Varun kept on yelling. He also announced his grudges against me.

'I think we can't form a good team and definitely can not be good friends. Just take your ass away from us; I would not like kicking it' Varun's words left a deep cleft in my mind. I was feeling humiliated.

I stood up and said, 'It's OK; I will get much better friends than you, you don't understand my problem. Just leave it; I also don't need such fake friends. Just go away and I dare you that no one can even touch me and my ass.' I banged the door on his face and left the room.

Suddenly the best buddies were no more together; we emptied the office that night itself and closed the website account.

I went to bed; I was feeling guilty but my hot temper overshadowed it and I decided not to talk to anyone.

I woke up early morning and saw Varun while I was going for a bath. We didn't exchange any words and publicly announced our differences.

I took an auto rickshaw to the hospital. The auto stopped at the same red light crossing; I looked out for the ragged girl to buy roses but she was not there. I came out of the auto and looked here and there but she and her mother were not there. I saw another flower shop; I purchased her favorite roses.

Many couples were roaming around; sitting in the park and enjoying the freshness of the morning.

'Everyone is in love; we should also fall in love' I thought.

'I have lost my friends and I don't want to lose her. I will marry her after I get a job. I will again speak out my heart to her and I know she is not going to say no today' my chain of thoughts was broken as the auto rickshaw reached the hospital.

I came out of the auto; looked at the sky and murmured, 'I will propose to her again today.' The cool breeze made me feel intoxicated with romance. I fell again in love with Vidisha.

I hid her favorite flowers behind me and entered her room. The room was empty and the cleaning staff was cleaning the room. I inquired about Vidisha but they had no answer.

Finally I went to the reception.

'Her family members came today and have taken her back. She has checked out' the receptionist showed me the signature of Vidisha.

'Do you know where she has gone? I mean which hotel? Has she given any contact number? She can't go without informing me......' I shouted at the receptionist.

'No, Sir we don't have any idea.' The receptionist said as the cleaning staff handed the key of room 55 where Vidisha had got operated.

'I found one letter there' said one of the cleaning staff. I took the letter from her and came out of the hospital.

I opened her letter.

'I am sorry; I have to leave without informing you. It seems that we will always meet and then part. Thanks for everything; I would not have survived if you hadn't stood beside me. You know when I said no to you and moved on with my life, I always thought of you; sometimes even missed you. Sometimes you have to stay away from your partner to realize the LOVE and I soon realized it. The more I tried to forget you; the more I started loving you; the more I cared for you. If love is all about caring about your partner; if it is all about sharing moments; if it is all about sitting beside the partner and helping her to come out of the malady; if it is all about small trifles and tussles then I must say I LOVE YOU. I am not going away from you today but I want to come back into your life with new happiness and new hopes. The time which we will spend apart shall make our love grow stronger; I know it will hurt but the time demands it. First you manage a good job and let me start my professional career and after that we will marry each other. I am leaving my e mail id; you can contact me through this.' I smiled as I had never thought Vidisha to be so responsible.

'I Love you....I will miss you.......Don't worry dude; you are allowed to flirt till the time I come back in your life. And then we will live happily ever after..........'

I folded the letter; kept it in my pocket and sat in the garden of the hospital. I didn't know whether to celebrate over my found love or to mourn over her departure. I found my lost love but I lost my best friends. I punched the air but again put my fist down in despair.

I tried to contact Varun but he always gave cold responses. I started mailing Vidisha regularly but there was no response from her side, probably she was still recuperating and had not joined her job.

After the bereavement of our friendship I was overcome by the feeling of boredom and aloofness. I started missing my friends. I had Love in my life but she was not in front of me; all this added to my woes. I was getting frustrated at not getting any replies to my mails.

'She probably made me happy while going; if she loved me truly she would have definitely replied to my mails. I helped her in overcoming this big accident and she just complemented it by saying, I love you...She doesn't love me truly; she loves me because I helped her in recuperating. I am just wasting my time by waiting for her' dark thoughts started coming to my mind. My friends, my love all had left me.

I found cigarette and drink to be my only friends in life which helped me in getting me out of my state of despair.

Meantime campus placements started in the institute. I wanted to have a job in the finance sector; I chose MONEY BANK profile as it was one of the best paying finance companies in the world beside the being 4th best investment bank in the world and I applied for the profile the company. I was just like any other youth who wanted money, fame and power in a short span of time. Finally the company came to the campus and I was amongst one of those ten lucky persons who got selected in the company.

I sent a mail to Vidisha about my newly found job and went out to booze with some friends. I took them to the biggest restaurant and bar in the locality. I booked two tables; after all I had been selected for a high paying job. People came in large numbers to congratulate me. I was surprised to see Varun joining my bash.

'Congrats buddy' Varun said.

'Thanks' I showed my attitude.

He took one shot of whisky and left. I came to know about his placement from some common friend. Varun got placed in some tech company; it was expected from him after all he was a tech savvy guy.

We boozed till late night.

I opened my mail box but it was empty; I expected a mail from Vidisha but she hadn't replied to any of my mails. I didn't know what happened to her. Suddenly her commitment; promises and her love were proving to be false.

The world came crashing down. Suddenly I felt all alone in this crowded world, due to which I was keeping a bad temper. Tanya was the only old friend who was in my life. But soon she also went away when I told her due to my bad temper that I didn't love her; but I could entertain her in bed. I don't know what made me react like this on Tanya's proposal of love. Probably I wanted everyone to go away from my life, after the departure of Varun and Vidisha from my life. I wanted to live a celibate life.

I had my farewell and finally left the Indian Institute of Technology and started my professional career which promised to bring a lot of wealth and fame into my life.

In just three months I was transferred to the head quarters of the bank in the United States and with the hope of becoming rich I moved towards the West. I liked the country side; I always wanted to be in such a country.

Back to the reality...... (at the shores of lake)

The ray of the sun fell directly on my eyes; the stream of water touched my feet and then just turned away from me like my luck. I opened my eyes to find myself in the present. It was my past full of friends, love and fun. And now I stood at the threshold of my future which looked dull. I didn't know how I had slept on the bench placed near the shore of the lake. I stood up; lighted my cigarette and started walking on the shore of the Powai Lake when suddenly my phone rang.

'Hey, what happened last night? Why did you go away?' Tanya was on the other side.

I love someone else and I am committed to her. My message was enough for Tanya to make her realize that I didn't like the way she liked me.

'O.K. Good for you.' She didn't even bother to inquire about the girl whom I loved and graciously ended the call. I realized that it was my last talk with Tanya; she won't talk from now on.

I took heavy steps towards the hostel. As I passed the Gymkhana and the ground I was reminded of my college days. Now it seemed like the walls, the ground, the people passing by, were laughing at me and my fate.

Life moves on...

I reached Rajeev's room. I opened my suitcase which I had kept in Rajeev's room before I went to join my job. It had all my certificates, accolades, few photographs of friends, few scribbled letters which I had written to Vidisha but never posted, few documents of JOBS MADE EASY and a bag given by my grand pa.

I was dejected; I had lost everything in my life. The pain was prolonged since I was loosing everything one by one, first Vidisha then Varun and then my job and now I am loosing hope to fight. This competitive world was really eager to swallow me.

'RECESSION' how could I forget this word; it took away all my happiness.

I opened the Times Ascent to search for a job; I was ready to do anything. Before I could move to the supplement, news on the front page caught my attention.

'RECESSION takes more life' said the article.

I glued my eyes to the article which said, 'After loosing his job from a big consulting firm in the U.S the man went on a rampage; gunned down his family and shot himself dead. The man was of Indian origin.'

It was not a war between two countries; it was not a natural calamity; it was not a global warming issue; it was not an issue of some dangerous virus spreading globally, neither was it the downfall of the President of the U.S. It was even more treacherous than a war, a natural calamity that had taken away happiness from many people's lives; caused many big companies and offices to shut down; made so many youngsters go jobless overnight, made many commit suicide and even kill their families; made many people lose their money on the stock exchanges. Can there be anything more treacherous? And it was spreading globally. I was not the only one who was affected; there were so many countless people thrown out of their jobs. Everything happened within a week after the debacle of the fourth largest investment bank. It was a FINANCIAL RECESSION.

I kept on reading the news paper and turned the page to find that a big Airline company declared sacking its thousand employees. But it had taken a political turn when the sacked employees went to the great politicians of India who rescued them and got them back their JOBS. It was a great drama for the media who surrounded the airline office and the politician's house. Thousands of people protesting made the news even more attractive.

For the next couple of days it was the turn of different sectors in the market to lay off their employees. All the companies said only one thing to their employees while throwing out.

'SORRY, it's RECESSION'

Soon the virus called RECESSION spread in the entire body of the world and many countries felt the heat and the only way for the companies to overcome it was to reduce the overheads by throwing out some people. Even the I.T sector which was a boon to the nation and had boomed like anything offering so many jobs was also crippled. The big players of Information Technology and even oil and gas sector suffered huge losses and kicked out many employees. There was complete panic everywhere.

Stocks rolled down with the speed of the score in a T20 cricket match; the index touched the lowest point, many banks declared bankruptcy. Thousands of people lost their money on the stock exchange. There was complete panic in the market and I was one of the victims of the virus called RECESSION.

The finance minister called for a press report and addressed the nation not to panic at such a turbulent time. 'We are working on it, our economists are doing the research; we will reduce taxes to compensate for the losses incurred by the common man' said the finance minister.

I opened an account with all the online job websites and portals. I tried to contact some managers of the companies. I applied to more than hundred companies for a job. I was willing to do any kind of job.

Finally I got a reply from an F.M.C.G company who were looking for an analyst. I took my resume and certificate file; removed the dust from it and took out my tie and suit and was raring to go.

My interview with the F.M.C.G company....

'Hello, Armaan. Nice to see you here. I hope your day was fine' said the interviewer.

'It's my pleasure Sir' I showed all my thirty two teeth to him. My behavior certainly impressed them.

'It will be nice if you offer me this position' I thought in my mind and kept my fingers crossed. The interviewer announced the general H.R round of interview.

'So tell us something about you?' asked the H.R manager.

I started off with my history, my histrionics, my achievements, accolades and why was I fit for this job.

'Besides having a good track record of academics and a financial job; one trait which stands out in me are my leadership and management qualities. I have held many posts during my college life and organized many events and coordinated with the corporate world. With such great experiences I am raring to go ahead in my life and I think I will do justice to this job' I said.

'I will definitely do justice to this job' I corrected my statement confidently. The interviewer was pleased to hear to that. My interview was going the way I wanted it to go.

There are only two ways to handle an interview either mould the interview in such a way that each and every word you speak impresses the interviewer and they ask whatever you want to say and the second is to keep on answering wisely defending your position. I tried the first one and it worked.

Then they started bombarding me with the general questions that are expected in every interview.

'What's your future plan?'

I laughed and said, 'I have been thrown out of a job last week and now I don't believe in future planning. What I can say is that I will work with excellence and will give my best shot in all the work I do and would like to take small steps everyday and would like to reach a higher hierarchy in the company.'

My answer was quite frank and for the first time I didn't use any diplomatic words, I was natural. The answer also impressed them.

Being natural and sticking to your strength always help in an interview.

'Why do you think we should hire you? Are you comfortable in extensive travelling? What's your strength and weakness? Where do you see yourself in the next five years?' the bombardment of questions continued.

I answered all the questions in the best possible manner; even the interview panel appreciated my answers and my talent.

'We are looking out for candidates like you in our firm who will take charge and lead the company to new heights' said the beautiful looking H.R, Shailja.

I smiled as I knew I have cracked this job.

'One final question' said the seductive H.R manager in her soft voice.

I smiled back and looked at her with all courtesy.

'Aren't you overqualified for this position?' asked the beautiful woman.

'My life has been rich with experiences, successes and failures. I have learned a lot from all kind of work I have undertaken and the best is yet to come. I will savor this job and it would open a new window of learning to me. I think I am qualified enough to compete for this job but no way am I overqualified. One life is too short to learn everything.'

Shailja appreciated my answer and I knew that I had got through. Just a formal announcement was left when suddenly the mobile of the C.T.O rang.

'Hello Sir' he said with all courtesy.

'But Sir????' he said.

'How??? From today' he replied to the anonymous voice on the other side of the phone. I was unable to understand this jargon.

'O.K Sir. I will do it' finally he cut the call.

'Let's moves, we have a meeting with the CEO' he announced to his employees.

'When will you give the results?' I hurriedly asked them as the H.R started packing her stuffs.

'Recruitment freeze. The CEO called us and said no fresh recruitments in such turbulent time.' the CTO said to me and the panel of interviewer left.

It was disheartening news for me; my interview had gone so well but still I didn't get selected. All my efforts, hard work failed.

'Is talent not recession proof?' I shouted at the other candidates sitting there for their turn to face the interview.

The receptionist soon placed a placard on the notice post saying,' RECRUIMENT FREEZE due to RECESSION' all the candidates dejectedly left the office.' She made a point to give a big smile to everyone to boost their confidence.

I was CRIPPLED and so were many people. I reached back to my room. For the next few days I kept trying for jobs without getting a single one. Finally I decided to go for Ph.D. and applied to many foreign universities. I never wanted to study but this was the only option available to me and getting Ph.D. from an overseas university was not an arduous task.

I was on my morning walk when I saw Varun.

'Hi, Armaan' he said.

We were talking after a year.

'Hello' we exchanged a formal smile.

'So what's up? What are you doing these days?' Varun asked me.

'Nothing, waiting for recession to get over and trying out for a new job' I replied and we started jogging.

'Hey let's drink together tonight. It has been long time since we sat together and enjoyed' Varun took long breaths and was feeling fatigued.

'O.K. Come to Rajeev's room.' I tried to end the bitter relationship between us.

Varun continued to his friend's room and I came back to Rajeev's room. Rajeev was also preparing for his interviews. Campus placements had started one month back and almost more than fifty percent remained unplaced and this was the case in all the institutions in India. Be it IITs, BITs, NITs, IIM s and deemed universities. Rajeev was brushing up the H.R questions which were expected in almost all the interviews.

I laughed as I saw Rajeev mugging up the answers.

'It's recession time, DUDE. You need to say everything right, if you mess up any answer you are gone' Rajeev said and kept on mugging his answers.

'You carry on. We will have some recession free alcohol tonight' I changed my clothes and left the room while Rajeev kept on brushing his skills.

'It's really strange. We hardly know our talents before an interview. It's only because of an interview that we do our personality survey and assign some heroics qualities to ourselves. What if we knew ourselves right from the beginning of choosing a career? Then probably we would have performed much better in our jobs and our qualities would have taken us to a much higher positions.' Strange thoughts appeared in my mind as I reached the wine shop.

'I would end the cold war between me and Varun' my mind swung to another issue in my life.

The clock struck 11 pm, I was waiting for Varun. Finally he arrived. I had already prepared a peg for him.

'Take this' I handed the glass of wine to Varun as soon as he entered the room. I clinked Varun's and Rajeev's glass with mine and celebrated the association of lifelong friends.

Only five pegs of wine were enough for Varun to blurt out his feelings.

'I am Sorry.' He said.

We looked into each other eyes.

'We should not have ended our friendship this way. We had been close friends for the last four-five years and had parted like enemies. I abused you, even cursed you; I should not have done this to you.' Varun was feeling guilty for breaking the friendship.

'Cheers' I winked at him and tried to lighten the moment.

We knew that the bond of friendship would blossom again. This was a long barren period of time when we didn't talk. We had so many small tussles before due to personal differences but we always shed our differences the next day and continued talking; enjoyed the friendship. Probably this was the longest time when we didn't talk and didn't even bother to contact each other. But today the things were a bit different I wanted my friends back in my life but I was feeling embarrassed in saying sorry to them.

'So how was your Job in the United States, a place where you always longed to go?' Varun asked gulping down another peg of wine.

'Oh..Don't ask man, it was going awesome until the bank declared bankruptcy' I played soft music on Varun's laptop.

'I came to know about your job loss from Rajeev. I really felt bad about it' Varun changed the music to his favorite Bollywood songs.

'Yeah, it was really difficult to digest but it didn't happen suddenly. The bank was not performing well since 2007 and if you believe the internal news then our CEO knew that the bank would close down due to bankruptcy. Even a few higher officers too knew about it. But they never let us know what was going on; they gave us a bonus, sent us to exotic places and suddenly the truth was revealed to the employees. Even in the interviews to newspapers they confidently declared that the bank had suffered losses but they were minor. The truth was hidden from the entire world, but the last month was too hectic for all of us. We worked 24*7 as the team leader gave us an indication of the huge losses of the bank and inevitably the bank closed down.

'Corporate world looks so charming and attractive from outside, but if you go to its root one can easily see the fraud cases of the company, their short term benefit plans and their empty promises. Major chunk of the company's profit is retained by the company and higher authority and what do you get in return for your hard labor? Some rupees or may be some foreign currency to keep you happy. These companies take the best chunk of students, from the best institutes, just name any (IIT, IIM, Harvard, Kellogs, and MIT) and you will find an employee from that institution. These employees are taught only one thing in their corporate office. How would you benefit the company in the shortest period of time? All companies want to have a huge profit in a short period of time, the managers devise such strategies so that they benefit at the earliest without seeing the future prospect and how would the plan fare in another three to four years. But you can't blame anyone; it's just inherited. Every employee passes it on to another. The entire policy should be changed if we want to see a stable market.' Varun sounded like an economist.

'Hey let's enjoy, why have you started with the history?' Rajeev clinked his glass with Varun's.

'So what are you doing these days?' I asked Varun.

'I am just sticking to my boring job of chemicals; fortunately they have not thrown me out till now.' Varun winked.

'Sutta hai kya?' Ankur came in with Vinod.

'Do you have a cigarette?' Ankur, the cartoon arrived with his favorite dialogue.

I knew he wouldn't compromise without gulping down a few pegs. Finally I did the honor and offered him a peg and a cigarette.

'It seems my entire old team is sitting here' Vinod said.

'I am sorry Vinod' I knew the company had closed down because of my negligence.

'No No, its OK. Just enjoy, it was not destined to happen' Vinod said.

'One thing I forgot to ask' Varun said in between.

'What?????' I asked anxiously.

'Where is Vidisha?' Varun inquired.

I gave a small smile, 'I don't know where she is. She is out of my sight. But she has promised to come back soon, I tried to contact her but there is no response from her side. But believe me I will marry her one day. She is out of my sight but not out of my mind.'

'She will always be in your mind, I know that.' Varun said, as Ankur left.

'But it's just like a movie where we are parting and meeting again.' I said.

Rajeev played the rock music at a high volume, we were all in an inebriated state and we didn't know that we had crossed the permissible decibel. Few students came and requested us to tune down the volume. But our low volume was also high for them. They complained to the security office of IIT in the night. It took them just fifteen minutes to reach the site. And then came a white Maruti van (security officer of the institute), a nightmare for all the students residing in the campus. The arrival of the van always led to DACA, disciplinary action in which students can also be expelled.

We were the alumni hence it didn't bother me and Varun but we were thinking of poor Rajeev, who had been caught because of us. But the security personnel were quite nice towards us and a fine of 5000 rupees was imposed on Rajeev and a 15 day ban from IIT was imposed on us as punishment. We left the campus that night itself.

We took a chawl in the suburbs of the city near Mulund.

I confided all my secrets to Varun and he did the same and we knew that we had always been good friends. We again started sharing the room but now in a claustrophobic chawl. We shared jokes, laughed on our lost job, played music and enjoyed as any other youth would have done.

'Hey, didn't you hook any American bombshell? Enjoyment without commitment as you always wanted' Varun asked risibly.

'They can be directed to bed for pleasure very easily. It's all legal there.' Vinod entered in.

'Even their red light girls are as beautiful as our page 3 babes' Varun continued.

'No man, I used to think that way when I was a teenager and until I fell in love with Vids. I can only say one thing; I am a cent percent virgin'

Laughter broke out amongst ourselves. I didn't think I narrated a joke to them.

'But I don't think that true love can exist in such a treacherous and a libidinous society' Varun was interrupted as his mobile rang in between our discussion.

'I think I can bring a change to society by being loyal to her. Common man, I love her. This is enough for me to remain bonded with her till my death.' Varun smiled as he received Rajeev's call very graciously.

We came to know from their discussion that Rajeev had again got drunk and was very upset after getting rejected by twelve companies.

'Be calm, you will get a job from the campus' Varun handed the handset to me.

'Don't worry dude, be confident. It's a bad time and whoever stays calm and acts intelligently will win the race. Now just sleep and be prepared for the next interview.' I sounded like an experienced campaigner; after all I was also a victim.

Rajeev almost cried and rang off.

'I wish this poor chap manages a job.'

'It's difficult at such a turbulent time.' Varun said.

'But it's not impossible' Vinod did not complement Varun.

'Is there anything in the market called recession proof?' Varun raised a small question which none of us could answer.

'Even the great talent which resides in great human beings is not recession proof. If the market is in boom even an intermediate passed student manages a job but if the market is down even a highly qualified person with a degree from a great institute does not find a job in the market. Why is it so? Does individual talent hold no importance for these companies or is it that one will get a job when every other person gets a job?' Varun raised national issues that would have challenged even the great debaters.

'I don't have a solution, but I want to fight, fight for my pride, fight for my career and eventually the best thing would happen.' I know this.

Vinod was silently listening to our discussion.

'You know the only solution to our problem is JOBS MADE EASY. Entrepreneurship is the need of the hour' Vinod spoke for the first time.

We preferred to keep quiet as Vinod continued.

'When spirits are low and market is down why not create a market of our own? Many businesses were started like this; it was the demand of the hour that time. Many unsuccessful people who didn't manage a job fought hard and opened their own ventures, they started on a very small scale and grew slowly and after a few years they became the market barons. We started our company as a mission which was never accomplished; now the time has come to shed the callowness of youth and change our own lives. Why are me depended on the market? Why not run a parallel business?' Vinod still had trust in me and Varun even after the failure of the company.

'And believe me at such a turbulent time people need online job portals and websites. So take a decision overnight; may be the only way to turn the wheel of fortune towards our self is to start the work from where we had left.'

I was reminded of a job website where I posted my resume for a job. Varun said and left us thinking.

I couldn't sleep the entire night, the sour memories of my past and our unsuccessful attempt haunted me. I could visualize the past in parts; I was reminded of my bitter relationship with my friends because of my negligence towards the company. Next morning I went back to the hostel to meet Rajeev and take my suitcase from his room. I was thinking of our company all through the way.

Finally I reached the hostel. The hostel gate was deserted. I found it quite strange as it was a favorite hangout for the couples. I climbed the staircase and reached the first floor. There was a massive crowd standing in the corridor.

'I am an asset to this institution' I smiled as I walked through the corridor.

I saw Ankur on the way.

'Need a cigarette to get charged up' I laughed and reached Rajeev's room.

The Dean of the institution was standing there. I smiled as I knew Rajeev would have certainly played some prank or must have played his surround system loudly or may be kicked somebody's gate or some body's ass last night in an inebriated state.

The Dean gave me a sharp look; I realised, the matter was something serious.

'Where were you last night?' the Dean posed a question to me.

I was in my room in Mulund.

'What happened. Sir?' I asked as I entered Rajeev's room.

I was terrified as I entered his room. His clothes were lying on the floor; books were torn and the pages were flying in the air.

'Rajeev committed suicide last night' The Dean finally broke the news.

I couldn't believe what he said, neither what I was seeing. Rajeev was lying dead on the floor with a rope round his neck. He hanged himself to death last night.

'He didn't come for breakfast, so I came to his room. His neighbor had complained of the music being played continuously since last night. I called on his cell but there was no response. I knocked repeatedly on his door but still there was no response. Finally we burst into the room to find Rajeev hanging from the ceiling' one of the witnesses said.

I called up Varun; he came immediately.

'A letter was also found along with the body' The Dean handed over the letter to me to have a look at it.

Everything had happened so quickly that we were not in our senses. I had never thought even in my wildest dream that a brave guy like Rajeev could do this. Tears started rolling down our cheeks.

'I should have come here when Rajeev called me' Varun cursed himself.

I opened the letter, 'I came to IIT with big aspirations, to find a good job and to support my family who spent a lot of money on my studies. But I am unable to get a job, I feel the pressure. And I know that I will not get a job this year and my family will crumble due to debts. I can't face them; I feel embarrassed for not getting a job. So I have decided to kill myself.'

Soon the ambulance and the police came and took charge of the body. The body was sent to Kanpur, Rajeev's home town.

Next day Rajeev's suicide hit many news paper, 'An IITIAN kills himself for not getting a job.'

We came back to our room. We had lost a good friend and a partner of our business. For next few days none of us talked about business. We preferred to be in the room.

'What the hell is going on?' I said loudly coming out of my sleep.

For the past one month I have been hearing such news; someone committing suicide; someone killing their family, and job losses. What has happened to the youth of our country? Why are they crippled?

'Even we have suffered losses but aren't we supposed to be fighting?' Varun said.

If the youth, who is the fate of any country is behaving like this then what will happen to the future of the country? I have seen youth like us who are trying to get back to normal life, making efforts and also youth who just waste away their lives.

We needed some magic in our lives, we needed a person who would change our mood, make us realize our potential, make us forget our past.

Rajeev's death left us all crippled, we lost our good friend. We wanted to start our business again and we had lost one of its members. Days passed, we were recovering from the shock, and no one talked about career and business.

I opened my mail box to check whether my luck had favored me in getting a job or a Ph.D. position. I found one mail from a very reputed institute of Europe. With excitement and eagerness I opened the mail.

Dear Mr. Armaan

To our utmost regret, we have to inform you, that we cannot accept your application for the Graduate School, Munich. Unfortunately, no position was offered to you by the group leaders of the CMSZH Graduate School. Please do not think of this as being a ranking of your scientific skills, as we were very much impressed and satisfied by the standards and level of your qualifications. We thank you very much indeed for your interest in the Graduate School of Chemical and Molecular Sciences, Munich and wish you all the best for your future scientific career.

With kind regards.

I gave a small smile on reading the mail; such kinds of mail were becoming very common in my life.

'I have lost but I have not been defeated', I smiled as I deleted the mail.

Finally we vacated Rajeev's room. I brought my suitcase and personal computer from his room. I opened my suitcase and the bag given by my grand pa.

'Believe in yourself and the world will follow you' he had said while handing this bag.

I never bothered to open it as I thought it would have antiques or some family pictures about which I was least bothered.

Finally I paid homage to my grand pa by opening his bag. I was surprised to find no such thing in that bag. It had just one big envelope.

I opened the envelope to find a few colored cards, I smiled.

It had four strips of colored cards on which something was written and probably had the solution to our problem. I wish I had opened this bag earlier.

'RUN' the yellow colored card said.

'EXPLORE' was inscribed on the red colored card.

'STRIVE HARD' boldly it was written on the magenta colored card.

'LEAD' the brown card said.

Probably this was the only solution to our problem. There was also a letter in the envelope. I took it out and started reading it.

'Here are the four colors of life which everyone should savor. If you follow all the four cards you will reach where you want. Success is not so easy to get; you should have a balanced mind with no fear and frustration in it. You should always be optimistic. I had lost so many battles in my life but believe me I lost but was never defeated. I came back with firm determination and won many accolades in my life. So be cool, calm and composed and strive hard for success.'

The guidance of the elderly had some impact on us. I took the four cards and stuck them on the wall.

We decided to move on with our lives and revamp our fallen business. I called on Varun and Vinod and we started working for one common goal- JOBS MADE EASY. Probably this was the only solution to our problem.

Love @ Recession

Varun and I went to the gymkhana of the society; the building had a dilapidated look and had an antique structure. But from inside; it was opposite. It had state of the art facility and beautiful modern chicks; came there to burn some calories but instead ignited men's passion by wearing short T shirts and lowers. We discovered a new place for us in the gymkhana, a red brick wall behind the long tennis court that looked like a more youthful and energetic place. A light breeze was blowing and it looked as if it would rain anytime. We sat on the bench, placed near the wall.

'So how is Vidisha?' Varun shot a question from nowhere; just like the tennis player on the court serving a perfect ace.

'I don't know........I am not in touch with her.' The players went away; probably their match was over.

We rushed towards the long tennis court on seeing it vacant. We hardly knew the rules of play but we always enjoyed it. We were just amateurs.

My dreadful serve hit the wall. Varun laughed on seeing it and in no time the ball rebounded from the wall and found Varun's head. It hit him hard.

"Smash......" he went to his knees and then to the ground.

I laughed and came running towards Varun.

'You naughty girl, I won't allow you to go today. You look so sexy today' Varun murmured.

I buttoned up my T shirt and moved a little away as I thought he had become a desperate gay in just three months.

'Your figure is just perfect.....I wish I could hold you in my arms' he added.

I looked at myself and found a lot of fat in my body.

'You sexy.......your b..bs....'Varun murmured as I emptied the bottle of water on his face.

'Where were you?' I asked him smilingly.

'Ohhh...What happened?' he asked.

The ball hit your head and you went into your naughty and wet dreams.

'Who is the girl?' I inquired from Varun.

Varun blushed and said 'ANANYA'

'Ohhhh.....great going dude and may I know about your love story?'

And Varun started off with his romance in the corporate world.

'I was sent to meet a client and give a presentation of the product but I had no clue that this will change my life and I will also fall in love.

It was just another day for me, full of work and no holidays. The stress of work was showing on my face, my boss noticed it; he decided to put me in the marketing sector for the next couple of months as he thought I was getting bored with the office work. And I was on my first assignment where I met this lady; three years older than me. I always wanted to be in the marketing sector but I never knew that it would be a ticket to hell and I would lose my job one day' Varun said.

'Are you nuts? You were seeing someone older than you? Do you think this relationship has any future? I mean your parents might have an objection.'

'When love happens, it just happens. Love is a game of heart and brain. When heart agrees, brain has to just follow it.' Varun philosophized.

The guy had changed in three months. Varun surprised me by disclosing his love affair. He started off with his short love story.

Three months back: Nariman point, Mumbai.

'I reached the office of this FMCG Company half an hour before as it was my first assignment and I wanted it to be perfect and impress my boss. The office was near the shores of the Arabian Sea and the sea could be viewed from the multistoried building.

I sat near the window, the fresh air from the sea made me feel divine and fresh.

Half an hour passed. The receptionist brought a cup of tea and informed me that the H.R is in a meeting with the M.Ds and C.E.Os; so could be a bit late. I patiently started sipping the tea.

Three hours passed away but there was no sign of the H.R manager. I politely inquired about the H.R manager from the receptionist; she called on the H.R extension number and said with a smile,' 'Sorry, Sir. Please wait for fifteen to twenty minutes more'

My patience was taking a toll on me, one hour passed and I was feeling perturbed.

Ignoring my job, I directly went to the receptionist and said to her, 'what the fuck is this? I am not a sales man or some sales representative. I also hold a good post. Your company called us for the presentation and your careless H.R has no time even to come up and show her bloody face and say, 'Please bear with us?' Fuck off...I am leaving. I banged the desk with the file kept on it and was about to turn and leave when a female voice interrupted me.'

'We are sorry Mr. Varun for keeping you waiting for such a long time, but we were caught up in a very important meeting. So I am extremely sorry, please bear with us' the female voice said.

I turned and was bowled over by the beautiful smile and face. She possessed a divine beauty and a body that could have made her enter into the tinsel town of Bollywood.

Suddenly I found my voice more smooth and my behavior, like a gentleman's.

'It's OK...Ma'am' I bowed with full respect.

She directed me to her cabin, I followed her obediently.

'Ohhhhh.......God..I have never seen such a beautiful and a soft spoken girl before,' I thought, as I sat in front of the divine beauty, forgetting that she was an H.R and was paid for her politeness and style.

'Hi, I am Ananya; the H.R manager of the company.' She gave a smile and shook hands with me.

'Actually I am sorry for the incident that happened outside.'

I didn't know why I was sounding so nice to her. I was kept waiting for four hours and just five minutes with this lady made me overcome those four tortuous hour.

'No, it was our fault....'Ananya showed all the courtesy of the H.R.

Finally I was brought back to the affairs of the office when she asked me to do the presentation of the product. I started off with my presentation and finished it a bit early as I had expected. I was unable to concentrate as I was falling for this woman.

'OK...I think your product is quite unique. I think we can have a deal.' Anaya said.

I looked ecstatically at her.

'So..........'suddenly I was at a loss for words off.

'What?' she asked.

I mean where do you live?' I didn't know whether it was an appropriate question to ask or not. But I continued with it.

'I live nearby....'She said as she didn't want to disclose her exact address.

'I guess Bombay is too big.....'I gave a smile.

Suddenly she broke into laughter, actually I live at Parel' she said.

'Ohhhhhhh.....What a coincidence even I live in Parel' I pretended as if I had the residence in the same society.

'It's already 5 pm now; can I drop you to your house?' I gave a proposal.

'No, it's OK. I will take a cab. And I don't want to give you more trouble as we have already given you by keeping you waiting for hours.' She smiled and probably understood what was going on in my mind.

'It's OK.....I am also going to the same locality and you have to wait for a while to catch a cab. Let's go and I am your client too.' I said risibly.

She got ready to go with me. I took my bike from the stand and she sat behind me very demurely. Now we started talking more about family and about ourselves. I was astonished to hear that she was an orphan, living with her uncle. Her parent died in a road accident. For the first time the busy traffic of Bombay seemed soothing to me as I was getting more time to spend with Ananya.

Suddenly it started raining from nowhere, I rushed my bike towards the corner of the street but by the time we could reach there; we were completely drenched in water.

We stood beneath an antique looking building, the road in front of it led to many coffee shops and above one of which was written,' *A Lot can happen over a coffee.*'

It was turning out to be an accidental and as well as an inevitable date. I smiled as I read that tag and took her to the coffee shop.

She opened a few buttons of her suit and opened her hair. My eyes remained wide open. I had never seen such a beautiful and unassuming lady. I was falling for her. Her expressive eyes, her beautiful lips, her smile, her beautiful face and her nature were attracting me.

Ananya didn't like when I addressed her as Ma'am.

Probably no girl or woman on this earth wanted to be called as a senior or superior in age.

We were talking like good friends.

She took me to her home. Her uncle was full of energy and didn't look as if he had retired. He had a very cool approach to life; he knew how to enjoy life even after retirement when most of the people spend their time under MRI scan. He probably had the perfect retirement plan.

After seeing him I was reminded of the advertisements on retirement solution plans where the ailing father was thrown out of his house by his son. The father was equally happy and said loudly, 'JIYO JEE BHAR KE' and thereafter he enjoyed his life, played and went for outings. The thought was lurking but still I managed to flash a small smile after being reminded of the advertisement.

Finally I met Ananya's cousin, a boxer by profession but had been dropped from the state team because of doping. He came on his big bullet bike; he had a perfect masculine look and a biceps 25 cms. He looked with a suspicious eye; linking me with Ananya.

'Hey Kid' he said.

I hate that three letter word but couldn't raise my voice against the giant.

I looked gently at him.

'Hey, are you thinking of some relationship with my sister?' he said.

'N.....No.....' my voice trailed off.

'Good.........' He said.

'She is a nice girl..........' I was stopped by the giant.

'Are you looking for a one night stand?' the heavy voice came hard on me.

'No..Not all...'my voice seemed choked as I was getting afraid of this giant.

'Don't even try to get near her; I will kill you if you do that' he said with a red eye.

Suddenly Ananya came from inside; I heaved a huge sigh of relief.

'Hey Bro, don't get angry, he is just my friend and our company's new client' she said and guided the giant brother to his room.

'Hey I am so sorry; actually my brother has lost his wits after being caught in the doping case last year. He was thrown out of the state team and since then he has lost his temper. But he is very sweet at heart.' Ananya said.

I was about to leave when Ananya handed me some document regarding the company's deal.

'What are you doing tomorrow?' I didn't realise whether it was good to ask this on the first day of our meeting.

'What....!!!!!!" she looked at me.

'I mean..........' suddenly I looked blank after seeing her brother at the window.

She kept on looking at me with a suspicious eye as if I was proposing to her.

'...............we can talk more of this company deal.....'I heaved a huge sigh of relief as I uttered all my defensive words.

'She gave a laugh and probably understood whatever I wanted to say.

Tomorrow is Saturday, a perfect weekend to spend with Ananya but I didn't have any courage to ask her for that, as her brother kept on peeping from inside the room and tried to hear our conversation. But Ananya surprised me.

'Hey, what are you doing tomorrow? We can talk more over this deal and your product. What do you say?' Ananya asked me.

'I wish I could be there...........'I gave a long pause 'but don't worry; I will be there at the coffee shop at 5 pm.' Ananya gave a small smile and went inside. Her brother kept on looking at me from the window and showed his 25 cms biceps. I rode away after seeing the giant.

COFFEE SHOP: the next day...

Now we were more like friends and she disclosed her many secrets. I came to know about her loneliness and her desire to get married but she didn't want to leave her uncle because she had to support him and an ill tempered brother who had lost his career after being found doping.

'So aren't you seeing any one?' I asked her.

She gave a smile, 'Actually everyone is afraid of my brother's temper.'

'What about you?' she asked me pointing towards my age.

'I am also single......'

'But at your age, love happens...'She said from her own experience and proving that I was just a kid.

I didn't want to argue over this, I remained silent.

I had a good job in hand; I was single and was saving a lot of money. So I had the choice to see a girl and luckily I had found one. But I never thought my age would create a problem for me, I had never fallen in love in my entire life and when I did fall, it was with a girl five years senior to me. But I always knew love sees no age. She narrated her story of how her parents had died in a road accident.

Soon after, we started meeting often, and started seeing each other. I took her for a date in a 5 star hotel. We had been good friends for the last two months and I thought of making a move ahead. Finally we delivered the product to the FMCG Company; the company had a tie up with ours for the product. My boss was very happy with me. I took advantage of our first success and took Ananya to a 5 star hotel. Money was not a concern for me when I was with her. I decided to propose to her.

I made arrangements for the special day, paid heavy money to the musicians of the hotel to play the best romantic numbers while I would be proposing to her. We ordered a sumptuous and costly food. Finally I donned some courage and pulled out a golden wrist chain from my pocket which I had bought for her.

'Hey, Ananya..this one is for the special lady in my life' I presented the chain to her.

She was completely astonished; she would have never thought even in her wildest dream that she would date a person three years younger than her. She blushed. I was completely bowled over by her simplicity, her charismatic smile and her feminine qualities.

'We have read in books; seen in reel life and often seen many couples. Love is blind, as they all say. It sees no age, no caste. And I confess my love to you. I want to marry you and live with you forever' I announced my love as the musician started playing a romantic number.

'Will you marry me?'

'Are you nuts? You are three year younger than me. It is not possible.' Ananya broke my heart in a second.

'I love you truly and age should not create any bar. And, come on, we are living in the 21st century; forget about what the society will think of us. It is me and you who can make our lives beautiful and I promise you a great future. I love you.' I went on my knees to propose to the angel of the contemporary world.

She blushed; I always knew that she had a soft corner for me.

'Will you marry me?' I revisited the famous Indian movie dialogue.

'Yes, I will..........' the voice echoed in my ears and I felt myself on cloud nine.

'But the only problem is my brother, you have to do something to impress him' Ananya said.

'Don't worry. It will be done' I said.

My next job was to impress this mad boxer thrown out of the state team because of steroids. I thought a gift was enough to impress the giant.

'What's this?' Vicky (Ananya's brother) opened the box.

He got really sentimental on seeing the gift.

'It had a pair of boxing gloves; some old pictures of Vicky when he had won a few grand slams and some encouraging words to make him jump back in the ring'

He held my arms and started crying, leaning on my shoulders. I had never seen this face of Vicky.

'You know I am made for this but I ruined it' he said.

'Boxers are fighters and fighters never give up, so whatever had happened is a past, now fight again for your glory and I know you will make it to the top one day' I said to him.

For the first time we hugged each other. He took me to the terrace and brought some beers along with him. It was a dark night, we drank till 2 am.

'You know I was never habituated to steroids but my performance was deteriorating. I wanted to be at the top and I found the wrong way out to increase my strength and capability. You know...I bought these steroids and some drugs from a vendor who sits outside the Dadar station.........'

Vicky slept on the terrace after talking about his past. Suddenly Ananya appeared before me.

She was in her night gown. She was looking very sexy and beautiful. The light breeze blew her air. She came right in front of me, her perfume was seducing me.

'Are you OK?' she asked.

Yes I am.

'I hope my brother didn't give you a lot of beer and I hope you are not feeling as intoxicated as he is.' Ananya gave a smile.

'I am feeling more than him; your eyes and your beautiful smile are making me more intoxicated.'

She gave her hand to lift her up.

I pulled her into my arms and suddenly we were feeling each other for the first time.

She drew her hands around me; I felt her lips on mine. We were in a very cozy position. I started kissing her body; she felt the intoxicating love.

She closed her eyes and presented her divine body to me. I held her demurely. She opened her eyes, looked into mine..........

'I love you........' she said as she locked her lips with mine.

My hand went to her waistline and notoriously opened the chain of her night gown. Her body was perfectly toned.

We were about to make love when Vicky made some movements, Ananya ran away on seeing Vicky's movement. I cursed Vicky for that.

The next day I took Anaya's entire family out for dinner.

We had been seeing each other for forty days and we hadn't realized how we fell in love. Ananya's uncle had some concern over Ananya's age so he decided to have a ring ceremony. But fate had written something else for us.

I never realized that I had become a spendthrift by that time and I was not paying attention to my job as well. One day I reached my office to find a letter on my table.

The letter mentioned that my job has been terminated because of the ongoing financial turbulence. My dreams were shattered and I felt like a big loser in my life. I cancelled my ring ceremony with Ananya as I was not earning any money and I always wanted to be financially independent.

'People say money can't buy love............But whoever said this was quite wrong.....Money can't buy love but money is required to support your love and your family. Money is not everything....It's true...But those who don't get it or lose it, for them, it is everything, a necessity'

The world came down hard on me. I applied for many jobs but I didn't get a single one. I was dejected.

I used to meet Ananya. I found the dhabhas a much suitable place for an unemployed person like me, Ananya didn't complain about it. She knew I would never ask her for any help. Probably we loved each other truly. But at the back of my mind I always thought that I was not the right guy for Ananya. She is so beautiful, financially independent and she could get a much better hubby than me; at least an earning one. Before recession I gifted her lot of things but now I didn't even have a single penny to buy some good clothes for her. Ananya's uncle was pressurizing her for marriage; her uncle received a proposal from some business man.

'You know what, Ananya.....I think we should part now and move on with our lives. You will get a much better person than me' I said to her, holding her hands.

'I love you and I can't imagine my life without you. You have brought so much happiness in my life. We will marry one day and I will support you till you find a new job....'Ananya looked at me with her innocent eyes.

I can't......I don't want anyone to say that I am living on your income. I am a man; it is my responsibility to give you happiness, wealth and everything in life. And I don't want to rob that happiness from your life. Please understand me.....

'I can't leave you like this......'she stood up from her chair and was about to leave the dhabha.

'I will come back and my love will never die. I will come back when I get a good job and I will restore all the happiness in your life.............'

'What? Where are you going? Are you leaving me?' she turned towards me.

'I love you...............' I had only one answer.

'I will wait for you and I won't marry anyone if you don't come back....'she cried.

'Our love will win.......'I handed a rose to her, kissed her forehead and just turned away with tears in my eyes. I didn't want to get sentimental, and I left. I changed my mobile number thereafter and never contacted her.'

♥

The red brick wall got illuminated because of the sun's rays falling on it. Varun looked little dejected after he completed his fairy tale.

'Don't worry Dude....You will marry her one day....' I said and we came out of the gymkhana.

We both had something in common, an incomplete love and a job loss. And we were trying to make amends for it. We were feeling crippled, all the attempts we made, simply failed. But we decided to enjoy this barren period of life by travelling, outings and fun. We decided to go to Goa for relaxing as we wanted a break from everything.

Our Hero: Another Youth…

Sometimes we don't have to look up to great freedom fighters of India, politicians or some stars for inspiration and motivation, sometime we find it in just any common man around us. And we certainly found one on the beaches of Goa, a person who made us laugh and enjoy during such a bad phase of our lives.

The shore of the beach was surrounded by bamboos; a lot of people had gathered. A huge set was laid there; it looked like there was some movie shoot going on. The set was surrounded by a rowdy crowd; they kept on whistling and shouting. We moved towards the set to have a glimpse of what was going on. I was always fascinated by the world of Bollywood and wanted to meet some stars. I thought I had a chance of meeting one of them that day. As we reached near the set, people started shouting. Almost every one of them was uttering one name. Some girls were uttering abuses against that name.

The light monsoon winds set the tone for a perfect evening.

High tides striking the shore of the sea; the splashing water making a sound.

'Abhi………Abhi………Abhi……………' the people kept on enchanting.

'Common bastard………..' the girls kept on uttering abuses against the dude.

We managed to peep in through a large rowdy crowd. Some reality show was going on.

'Welcome back to I AM A STUD.......................' the host of the reality show appeared ecstatic.

It became clear to us that it was just another reality show in the harsh real world; every channel adopted this theme of reality shows to gain TRPs. But anyways it was better than emotional family soaps.

The rule of the reality show game was that on each day two participants will be sent out of the show which will be decided by consensus voting amongst the participants. Each day a task would be given to each person and half the candidates would be on danger line and the other half, who could do the task in less time than the other, would be on a safe line.

'So Abhi and Kunal have made it to the grand finale. Before we start the grand finale round let's see how the journey of these two young lads began.' The host of the show shouted and suddenly the lights were put off and a short movie started running on a an LCD screen.

The people kept on shouting and cheering for their unsung hero, Abhinandan (Abhi). The screen showed glimpses of romantic scenes of Abhi with the female participants. He romanced all the six girls present in the reality show and ditched all.

'Boooooooo........Booooooooooh..........'The female participants standing near the projector kept on shouting after seeing their own hot glimpses.

'We are just friends...........We are just normal friends.........Nothing is cooking between us........' all the girls said on the screen.

Abhi was acquitted of having sex with one of the participants; the screen led us to a dark room where one girl was sleeping alone. A guy came in and started discussing the elimination round. He suggested some name for voting out when his hand suddenly went on her cheeks and he started touching them. The girl also looked like a slut, kept on blushing and directed Abhi to her cheeks when suddenly everything became blurred. Next day the girl was charged of having sex and then there was all chaos. A lot of political lobbying was done by the participant to get saved from being voted out but Abhi was the smartest; knew how to tackle the situation. He approached Ria, another bombshell and started flirting with her. And this was the way he kept on escaping vote outs. He sometimes swung away and supported the boys' fraternity.

He kept on ditching everyone; made fake friends on the reality show. He fought with some participants, boasted of his physical strength and took everyone by surprise in the task. He was always on the safe line.

Suddenly the light on the screen dimmed and made way for Kunal, the other participant. He was totally different from Abhi. The short film presented him like an honest player none of whose moves was deceptive. He never duped any one, he knew the only way to survive on the show was to perform. And he did exactly that without the help of politics. Abhi always knew that Kunal was the only participant who would run him to danger and he tried many times to get the lad out of the show but Kunal was lucky because all the girls had their own personal differences and wanted to eliminate each other. Kunal was also on the safe line and never went to the danger line.

The short film was over and the proceedings were brought back to the beach. All the participants were called to see the grand finale.

'You searched for it everywhere...........' said one flex hung in air.

'But HELL is here..............'said another.

Kunal and Abhi came in. The girls started abusing Abhi.........

Abhi blew some kisses on the participants wearing short jeans. The female participants gave Abhi a tough look which hardly bothered him and he continued on his way.

'Abhi and Kunal..This is your final round........The one who wins it will take 10 lakh rupees and the prestigious title of 'I AM A STUD'..So are you ready for the final round?' The host looked into their eyes. Abhi and Kunal nodded their heads.

But wait a minute; the host gave a long pause.

Can you read that flex for me. The host told Kunal to read it for him.

'You searched it everywhere........' Kunal said.

He pointed Abhi to read the other.

"But the HELL is here..............' Abhi shouted loudly and gave Kunal a tough look.

'So coming back to the show...As I already told you the best man will win today. You reached here because you did well. But you have to do exceptionally well to win this. As the flexes say HELL IS HERE.........' The host moved to the centre of the set where two big holes were dug.

This is your task; the host announced looking at the 10 feet deep hole.

'Confused.........' He said laughingly.

You have to get yourself buried in this; there might be some craps inside the ditch. And the one who spends ten minutes inside this and comes out on his own, will win the game. It is as simple as this. The host announced the starting of the much awaited final.

Abhi and Kunal jumped into the hole, sand was poured on them. And after a minute, the hole was filled with sand. A pipe was bored along the holes, if any candidate felt suffocated; he could pull it from inside since one end of the pipe was bored in the hole, but by doing this he would lose the game.

The audience kept on looking at the two holes with their fingers crossed, it was dangerous but a very easy way to gain points on TRPs. Suddenly some craps started coming out from inside the sand. The game was getting dangerous.

The anxious ten minutes passed away. Suddenly there were some movements on the beach. People started shouting again. Majority of the people were supporting Kunal because of his clean image in the show.

The movements became prominent and the people started shouting.

Suddenly there was an upheaval on the shore and someone came out from inside with such intense force that the sand particles started floating in the air. There was a sandstorm for few seconds.

People rubbed their eyes and opened it to see the winner. I did the same.

Abhi was standing in front of everyone. His fans started hooting and praising him. He waved to his audience and fans and suddenly ran towards the other hole and started digging the ground.

Kunal was lying unconscious in it, he brought him outside and gave him some water. Finally Kunal opened his eyes. They hugged each other and Kunal congratulated Abhi on his coveted win. Abhi was not at all that bad, he looked like a decent human being.

This was the first time we saw this maverick. His body language, his diction, his expressions, his overall persona deserved great praise. He was well built, looked street smart and was loquacious.

The show was over; Abhi got the cheque. There was a small open air dinner party arranged for these participants. Varun and I congratulated Abhi and proceeded to our hotel and in no time we dozed off.

I felt an urge to have a cigarette, rose from my bed and went outside the hotel to find a cigarette shop. Finally I got one; while returning I saw a guy sitting at the shore. It was another bright morning with sun rays coming down hard on the earth. I went near that guy and was surprised to find that it was Abhi. We exchanged a smile and I sat beside him.

Abhi was doping. I was surprise to see him in such a state.

'So, what are you doing here?' I gently asked him

'Enjoying my life and my drink' he said, with a big smile like that of a sales representative who knocks on every other door and offers lucrative deals.

'So what do you do? I mean as profession' I asked him.

'Fun, Fun and more fun...........' He said.

I smiled and I wished that I could be like him too. I wished I could forget all the mishaps in my life and live my life like this guy.

This was the first time we introduced each other.

'Do you want to have the ultimate pleasure in life?' He asked me suddenly.

I thought that sex was the only ultimate pleasure for a man but this guy changed my views.

'And what is that ultimate pleasure?' I asked him courteously.

'It's not Sex as I can see from your roving eyes. Its DRUGS and the chemicals that make you feel heavenly', he said.

'Are you nuts? It kills....' I retaliated.

'But believe me it's better than a girl who comes in your life with an expiry date and leaves you in a wretched condition and you become ill tempered. Try it, it's better than a woman', he said.

He had his own homemade theory and he defended his act quite smartly.

'Believe me it's the best thing you can have in your busy and tense life', he said, gulping down his last peg of wine.

I gave a small smile and moved to my hotel. Abhi waved me from his bike while I continued walking to my destination.

As soon as I entered the reception room, I saw Abhi lying on the sofa. He was probably staying in the same hotel. I exchanged a smile with this young star.

'My room no. is 55, drop in sometime. We can have a drink together' He said and left for his room.

I reached my room in the hotel; Varun was packing his stuff.

'What happened? Where are you going?' I asked Varun.

'Let's go back; Vinod has called us back. I think we can have a big deal with an institution', Varun was still busy packing.

'I am not coming today; I want to extend my break a bit more. I will join you after two days.' I kept my wallet on the table and moved to the wash room. Varun followed from behind.

'Are you nuts? Let's go' Varun said from behind.

'I will come after two days, please let me have a break for two more days.' I said.

Varun didn't say anything and he knew that my losses were big enough. The only way to come back to life was by taking a break.

'If possible do meet Ananya, she must be waiting for you', I said to Varun.

Varun didn't reply and left the room. He still loved her and his silence would always speak against him.

I directly went to Abhi's room. He was listening to some pop album song and was singing along with it. I had never seen such a carefree, exuberant, maverick and a fun loving guy in my life. I wished I could imbibe some of his qualities.

'If I were like him; I would have enjoyed my life even at such a time of distress.' I thought as I exchanged a smile with Abhi.

'You want to have the ultimate pleasure in life?' he said risibly.

'Yes; why not.' I said as we came outside the hotel.

We drove away on his bike. He jumped all the signals that came in between and was hardly bothered for the law and order.

'*Bahen ke.....Laws* and order can't stop me' he gave a big smile.

He was definitely a truant and a maverick.

Finally after driving for an hour we entered into a small slum near some beach. I didn't know where he was taking me; I was getting scared of the place. Probably it was a brothel.

He stopped the bike near a dilapidated house; it looked like some old garage which had been closed now. Water was falling from its roof. Few unknown faces were outside the house, and they looked like bouncers.

'Hey Abhi...' one of the bouncers said in his heavy voice.

Abhi shook hands with this giant as we entered into the gloomy path that led to the staircase. We climbed the staircase and entered an illuminated room. It was quite the reverse of what it looked from outside. The room had a small pub and lots of foreigners were sitting in the room; drinking, smoking and kissing each other. And on the other side of the room few people were doping.

Abhi clinked his glass with mine and in no time we also started drinking and reached a state of high.

'You know what; you are totally opposite from what you look.' I mean you are the winner of a reality show; people recognize you as their hero. And you are wasting your life by doing such acts', I didn't know why I gave him this free knowledge.

'You know; I have a deadly past. My father wanted me to take over his dhaba business in Punjab but I always wanted to be an actor and I ran away from my home; came to Bombay only to find no place for me in this tinsel town. I started hitting gym; I joined an acting school. I always knew my potentials and capability. And one day luck favored me; I got a call from a leading production house. But they wanted me to invest fifty percent of the money in the film. I took loans, took money from my dad. I knew that I would repay them after the release of this movie. But suddenly one day I tore my ligaments while hitting the gym and the movie was on the floor already. The producers gave me fifteen days time to recover and I couldn't recuperate in the given time span. They cast some other actor in the movie and the movie is about to release now. My dad went bankrupt and the people from whom I had taken loans started cursing me. And in this way I lost everything in my life. But from that day I decided that I will not cry about my losses but will enjoy all these barren days.' Abhi gulped down the entire bottle of Vodka.

The intoxicating drink started commanding him and he reached a state of high.

'What about you?' Abhi released all the smoke on my face.

'I am just another youth caught up in recession. I have messed up my life; lost my job and am struggling to find a new one. I have lost the love of my life too.' I sounded a little sentimental to him.

'I have heard about recession in the news but I don't know what it is.' Abhi was an ignorant youth who was hardly bothered to know about India's GDP growth, inflation rate and recession. He was carefree and probably was too happy or too busy in his personal life.

'It's just a financial turbulence and a slowdown of Indian economy' I said it in a layman's language.

'Oh...Baden de...When did this happen?' He asked me anxiously.

The news of recession was hitting all the news channels, news papers and people were suffering and this moron didn't even know when had this happened. I preferred to keep quiet and we started boozing again.

'And where is the girl?' He broke the long silence between us.

'Don't ask about her. I love her madly and I am in search of her.'

He read my sentimental face which was full of emotions.

'Ahhhhh....come on man. Even I had a girl friend. She was always with me; she loved me a lot. She was elegant and even more elegant on bed. And when that movie went out of my hand; she also went away. No girl likes to be with an unsuccessful guy, there is nothing called love in this world. The opposite sex gets into a relationship to quench their lust; it's nothing more than an emotional drama where guys are duped by the external beauty. She doesn't understand your failure; she is with you when you are successful but when you are not, she speaks about compatibility and supporting her. My girl was a bitch; she is now seeing some other guy and every girl in some sense is a bitch' Abhi chucked the glass so hard that it broke into pieces that reached every corner of the room.

I tried to give some solace to this maverick.

'You know my love is incomplete till now; we are destined to meet one day as it has occurred in the past. She even likes me but our destiny has somehow made us part. But we love each other truly.'

'May be...But believe me love is the most dangerous game people have ever played in their life.' Abhi rose from his chair and entered another room. I followed him

The room was full of smoke. The air was intoxicated with chemicals and drugs. I never thought that this guy would prove to be a drug addict. Abhi sat beside a dark complexioned guy who looked like a West Indian. He gave something to Abhi wrapped in paper. Abhi gave five thousand rupees to this dark complexioned giant.

A lot of people were consuming drugs and chemicals and a number was playing in the background.

'We are partying.............We are partying.......'

The people kept on dancing on the number.

Sighing.........

Abhi took out some liquid on a spoon. I was not able to make out. He unfolded the wrapped paper and pour the powder on the spoon into the viscous liquid, started mixing it with his finger till the mixture became homogeneous. He took out a syringe; and sucked the entire liquid which was now mixed with powder. He injected the liquid into veins of his right arm. He sighed and after injecting the liquid he fell on the ground like a freely falling object. I ran towards him to help him.

'It's the ultimate pleasure one can have' he was enjoying that chemical which was now running in his blood.

'And the fun goes on.........' the song kept repeating.

Winces......

'Why don't you try this? You will forget all your miseries,' Abhi passed the wrapped paper containing the powder to me.

'Are you mad? You will die if you do this. This is dangerous', I shouted at Abhi but he was intoxicated and kept on smiling.

He kept on sighing.

'We would have injected vitamin C only if it were made illegal.' He said and kept on injecting some foreign materials.

Everyone in the room was injecting some chemicals inside their bodies. These were the spoilt youths who hardly thought of the consequences and were not bothered about their families, nation or even themselves. Suddenly I saw two men who were kissing each other; this was the impact of these drugs. People couldn't even identify the same sex.

One of the guys gave a long lasting smooch to his male friend. The other guy opened his shirt and directed his partner to his chest and they kept on kissing each other. Even girls were sitting over there; they were laughing like other guys but these guys continued their sex.

Guy is a wrong word to use; they were GAY.

'Are you people mad? You are spoiling your life; you all are stupid' I said to Abhi.

'We are not that fucking stupid.

Can't get a girl, no chance of a ride.

Got a girl, too much hassle.

You have to worry about bills, food, girl friend, job, family, your pet, your bike and about some cricket team that hardly wins World Cup. About human relationships and all those things: they really don't matter when you have got a sincere and truthful junk habit. I could offer million answers, all false. The truth is that I am a bad person.' Abhi retaliated.

'Take the best orgasm you ever had in your life, multiply it by thousand or even more and you are still nowhere near it. So just try this dude, you may forget all miseries of your life in a second' Abhi continued injecting the powder into his veins.

Probably he was right and there was no harm in trying it. I had already lost many things in life and I was just running after them to get them back. I thought of trying these chemicals.

I took the syringe from Abhi and injected into my vein and I felt like never before. I felt like I was flying in the sky and there was no gravity which would pull me back. I could see Vidisha standing in front of me in a beautiful pink suit. I rubbed my eyes and looked again, to find no one there. It was just a hallucination caused by the drugs which I was consuming. I still loved her madly; her thoughts and sweet memory still filled my heart.

I fell on the ground due to the intoxicating chemicals, I couldn't feel the gravity; my head kept on spinning and I felt like never before. It was certainly dangerous but who bothered. I was anyways a failure.

'I am broken from inside; I don't want to live. I have lost everything in my life. I wish I could find my love and marry her. I would be a happy man then. Her smile and her touch could blow away all the pain and unhappiness from my life. I wish I could see her again' my voice almost broke away.

Abhi tried to abate my frustration and handed over a cigarette.

The room was awash with drugs, that one could have for unhappiness and pain and these people consumed all. After all it was not that bad; an excuse which every addict has.

I too started consuming drugs. It became our day to day habit and we spent our savings on it like anything. After a few days I started feeling an urge for those chemicals in my blood.

We took morphine, dimorphine, cyclozine, codeine, temazepam, nitrazepam, phenobarbitone, methadone, pethidine, pentazocine, nalpubmorphine and dextromoramide.

Almost all the drugs selling illegally in the market were in our blood. Now I was not worried about anything in life and definitely not about a job. I was enjoying with my new friend, Abhi.

I woke up with a hangover. Abhi was sitting in front of me.

'Good morning' he said.

I exchanged a smile with him when suddenly he threw a bag at me.

'Let's move on....' Abhi started moving towards the door.

'What happened?' I asked him.

'We have to leave the place now. We are going to find her.' Abhi said as he unlocked the door.

'Find whom?' I asked.

'Vidisha' he smiled.

I came out of the hangover in a second on hearing that name.

'Are you nuts? How can we find her? I don't know where she works; and where exactly she lives. I just know that she is from Kullu', I splashed my face with water.

'I saw your agony, your pain last night. You love her madly and let me do one good thing in my life.' Abhi went outside leaving me alone in the room, with thoughts hovering in my mind.

'I packed my stuff and came outside', Abhi was sitting on his bike.

'Are we going on this?' I asked him.

'Two thousand kilometers is only what we need to travel. We will complete the journey in two days and we will take some break too after covering a few kilometers,' Abhi started his bike and we started our journey.

I always wondered about the ebullient and energetic nature of Abhi. He would be perfectly suited for a 24*7 MNC job.

In search of Love & Life

We started our journey. I was filled with the memories of past life; full of love, friends and betrayal always haunted me. I wanted to put everything back on track; I was in search of my life and my love. I wanted love to overcome all sorrows in my life; a medicine that can cure anything. I was broke, I needed love.

Abhi kick started the bike and in no time his left leg struck fifth gear and the bike was talking with air. He always knew that he was breaking all the rules.

'You are not a good citizen' I said from behind.

He gave a big smile after breaking another traffic signal but he was not the only one. When one is young, everything is taken for granted.

'Yeah...but who cares; what did I get when I was a true citizen who always knew what a loss was; who always followed the law and order? This is India man; people just die after struggling here. They don't even get food, cloth and a shelter to cover them; the big political talks of our politicians always fall short and they hardly do anything after winning. Even if they do; the money which they send for the development of the state goes into the pockets of corrupt leaders. And the opposition party criticizes it but they would have done the same thing if they had been at the center. Poor are becoming wretched; rich people and business tycoons are increasing their wealth and we the common youth are just fighting for our survival. Someone doesn't have a job; he is worried for it. Someone is not happy with his boss, wife and family; a few are unhappy with the working of the government, tension of family, survival and life haunts everyone. But I am happy; I am being selfish. I do whatever I like and believe me I am happy too.' Abhi sounded sensible for the first time.

'You have so many problems with your country why don't you raise your voice' I replied aggressively.

'Nothing can happen here; this is India. No one can change the system but everyone can adjust to it. And I am not a social worker who cleans up the society; I am just like any other person like you who wants to be content in his life; have a happy family, wife, children, home and money. And I don't want to be a lone fighter. How many people actually care for the country? Do you?' Abhi retaliated.

I didn't have any answer and I preferred to remain quiet.

'If you had not lost your job, you would have been in America, counting dollars, having fun and trying to get a green card. Did you ever think about your country?' Abhi said something which was definitely true.

'Come on; these are just stuffy text book material. If our politicians are not doing their duty with perfection then why are we acquitting each other? We have a democracy; we caste vote as a sincere and truthful citizen. We decide our government and it is now up to them to function in a desired manner. This is what we expect from them; and we sincerely look up to them that they would change the fate of a country which has been tagged as a developing nation.' Abhi continued.'

I had never thought even in my wildest dream that this guy who was so carefree, would talk like this.

'I guess my children would also hear that India is still developing or even my grandson. We will always be a developing nation but never a fully developed country in the real sense.' Abhi gave a smile after hearing me.

'We were young blood; we want everything to be done in haste.

'We need some young politicians; a youth cabinet.' Abhi declared.

'Why don't you join it?' I said as I was confident about the strength of this guy.

Suddenly he stopped the bike.

'What happened?' I asked him; I thought he got angry.

'*Bahen de.......*' he showed his little finger and rushed towards the bushes to empty himself.

He came back with a big smile.

'Are you serious? Do you think that a loser like me and a drug addict will be a good leader? Come on man; I am happy this way and I don't want to get myself dirty by entering into politics,' he sat on the back seat.

I kick started the bike and started driving it. We were speeding on the highway.

Abhi unfolded a piece of paper; it again had some white powder. The guy took more powders and cigarettes than food. I was getting anxious about his health but he hardly paid any attention to it. He asked me to stop the bike.

He took a piece of paper; spread the powder on it and started inhaling it. He bent forward; his eyes became red. He couldn't even stand properly. He was intoxicated. He sat on the back seat and I started driving again.

He kept on singing and uttering abuses on the people moving on the road.

'I wish I could enjoy my life like you.' I said.

He smiled.

'When one is a kid, one wants to grow up fast and join school. When one is in school, he wants to move further and longs to be in college; when in college he wants to have a bike, a girlfriend, and sex. Soon he wants to move on in life; one is itching to join a job and when he joins it he desires to get married and have a family. And when he marries he wants to have a kid and a perfect home. Soon one desires to retire, and when he retires he wants to be with his family. Life suddenly becomes dull; eventually after growing old he wants to die. And before dying suddenly he realizes he has never lived a life, never enjoyed it. He did whatever every other individual had done in life; never made his life special. So I want to do whatever I like doing, live my life like a maverick. Who cares for the fucking laws? I want to live like a king and do whatever I feel like doing. I may be sounding abnormal, but this is what I am. Who cares about the nation? I am happy because I exist. I have seen the lowest phase of life; have gulped them down with a sad face.' Abhi replied.

His reasons and demands were unique and not what society had laid down on him. I always thought of myself as a loser but this guy was changing my views.

The hot sun was melting into a cool night. The place was becoming dark. We decided to take a break in the journey; we stopped the bike at a dhabha and decided to take rest for the night.

After having sumptuous chicken curry and tandoori roti we decided to sleep in the open air. The dhaba had 2-3 beds placed outside. Abhi jumped on one bed and in no time, fell asleep.

I kept on looking at the sky, the stars and the ambience around. And in no time I also went into my dreams.

We were close for the first time and could feel our breath. Vidisha never behaved like this; she was taking long breaths and was afraid. I held her hand demurely, she turned away. I took the initiative; and kissed her cheek. She was feeling uncomfortable and shy like any other Indian girl. I could feel her feelings but at the same time she was getting passionate and wanted to come out of her goody family image and wanted to show that she had always desired to have sex. We decided to take a walk together.

'I am getting late' Vidisha said.

'Come on, only thirty minutes more' I smiled.

She was obedient like always.

We reached the sea shore. The cool wind blew her hair and the high tides, the blue sky and the shops near the shore made it a perfect romantic place.

She held my hand for the first time and we started walking along the shore with water touching our feet. She felt relaxed and very happy as the water touched her feet. She smiled; kicked the water with her feet. Water splashed all over.

Suddenly a big tide rose in the sea and came towards us. Vidisha got scared and for the first time she held me. The tide passed away, I touched the water with my hand as if exchanging hands and saying thanks to the tide which made her come closer to me. The tide died away but our passion couldn't die.

'I want to protect you from all misfortunes and all evils,' I said.

Vidisha moved away as the tide died on our feet.

She blushed but the response was too warm. But still I was an obedient lover.

We continued walking along the shore; I held her hand after donning some courage.

She ran towards the food court after seeing her favorite food being sold there. She was enjoying her *panipuri*. I kept on watching her.

'I love you...' I said looking into her eyes.

Her eyes remained wide open.

'Will you marry me?' I announced my true love.

She squirted out all the liquid which was inside her mouth and started laughing.

'I am serious' I said.

She kept on laughing.

'I love you' she tried to mimic me and started laughing again.

I looked at her with a serious face.

'It's too early to take a decision; you like me and I consider you a good friend. Even I have some feelings for you but let's be together for some time and if we are comfortable then you might, you know. YOU CAN MARRY ME....Just imagine how lucky you will be', she again started smiling.

'Yeah, and just imagine. We will have a family, our kids and a home. We will grow old together; will share our happiness and pain. I will be fatigued after coming back from office; your smile and your touch will make me feel fresh. I will love you till my death.'

'Oh....wait...wait.....' Vidisha intervened in between.

'I am getting late; let's move now. You can dream even in the autorickshaw,' she said and flashed a beautiful smile.

Bombay weather could be so unpredictable. It started raining again. We ran to take an autorickshaw but by the time we could get it, we were completely drenched in water.

We finally sat in the claustrophobic auto rickshaw. Vidisha shook her hair, splashing water on my face and looked like an angel.

We were good friends; I used to tell her about my crushes and she would scold me for being silly. She used to tell about her crushes too. She took me to the temple and classical music concerts and I would add them to the list of things she owed and then I would pounce back with a date.

The watch showed 9 pm.

She almost cried on seeing her watch.

'I am again late. Now I have to go to my friends flat as the hostel would be closed', she gave me a tough look as if I was the reason for getting late.

I gave a big smile on sensing that she would be with me for another hour.

"You like putting me in these situations, don't you?" she said.

"No. That's not true. I love putting you in these situations!"

That invited a punch on my arm.

And though I never let it show, I must say that she punched pretty hard.

It was our usual habit to fight over small things. We started taking a stroll near her hostel. She called her friend to take shelter for the night.

We continued walking on a path illuminated by moonlight; the walk was divine.

She kept on blaming me and was afraid of her family.

I held her hand and pulled her towards me. She kept on looking at me and in no time I kissed her lips. She pushed me away and went out of my clutches. Probably this was the only way to keep her quiet.

She turned away from me; I went near her.

Everything was happening in a small park near her hostel.

She suddenly turned and gave me a long smooch. I couldn't believe what was happening. I just closed my eyes to feel the divine feeling of love.

'I will always love you.' I whispered.

'I miss you so much.'

The feeling of love and romance was overcoming me. First kiss, first college, first love, first car, first bike and everything which comes first in life is always memorable, especially, first girlfriend and her first kiss.

I opened my eyes; everything was blurred in front of me.

There was no one in front of me. Suddenly she disappeared like an angel. I ran towards the road; inside the park; frantically I searched for her but she was not there.

'Vidisha............' my voice echoed and died in the streets.

My eyes moistened, voice became dull and I fell on the road.

Suddenly there was a big noise.

'A bottle hitting a car, a monstrous laugh, a car toppling and a girl coming out of it blood stained...Everything became silent for a while..'

'Ahhhhh..................' my sleep was broken by my chain of thoughts. It was just another nightmare.

I rose from the bed; took a stroll on the gloomy road. She was hitting my dreams every other night. I loved her madly though I never showed it to anyone after coming from America, that I was missing her badly. She was the only reason behind my existence; she always came in my dreams; boosted me up when my spirits were low and gave me confidence to move on in life. I would have easily given up life and would have chosen drugs over life but she was the only reason that kept me sane and breathing. I wish she comes in front of me once again and I would never let her go from my life.

Suddenly my phone rang.

'Hello.....Varun......'

'Hey, there is one bad news.' He made his point instantaneously.

'Another bad news. I am getting accustomed to it now. Just break the suspense now.' I sat on the bed.

'The landlord has given us a notice to vacate the flat since we haven't paid the last month rent. And the bill of our credit card is mounting too. The bank will soon block our credit cards and will send some bouncers to collect the money. Nothing is going our way.' Varun was serious.

'I will be coming back in two days; I will try to manage some money from my friends.' I tried to give some solace to my old chap.

'Y...Yeah..I hope things get better otherwise we will be screwed.' Varun said.

'Don't worry dude. Life will be normal soon. Hey, what happened about that investor was planning to sponsor our start up?.' I tried to change the topic of our conversation.

'Hmmmmmmm.....He has called for a meeting next week, so do come back soon. Don't commit the mistake which you did last time. This is our last hope to revive this company and our life.' Varun reminded me of my past.

'Don't worry; I will be there this time. Tomorrow I will meet

Vidisha and would declare my love and would come back. After reviving our company I will marry her and then we will be back to our normal life.' I smiled.

Varun gave his best wishes and finally ended the call.

I was lost in memories of Vidisha. I will declare my love tomorrow; I know she would not refuse my proposal. She has feelings for me.

'But what if her parents disapprove of this relationship? No one wants them daughter to marry a jobless person like me. And what if she refuses my proposal? We spent money like spendthrifts, never thought of saving money. What if my friends refuse to lend me money? And the worst could be the investors not turning up.' All pessimistic thoughts surrounded me.

I cursed myself, unfolded the paper kept near Abhi. It was some drug; I emptied it on my hand. I lost everything from my life. I started inhaling the intoxicating powder. My coveted job, my love and my friends had gone away from me. Suddenly the powder made me reach cloud 9, I reached the inebriated state in no time, looked up to the sky and closed my eyes.

I opened my eyes to find Abhi standing in front of me.

'Come on man, we are getting late. Look it's already 10 am' Abhi shouted it me and pick started his bike.

I went and sat behind him on the bike.

'So you emptied my last medicine. That was all I had,' Abhi said as the bike started talking with the air.

'Medicine....What's that?' I exclaimed. I was still having a hangover after the powerful powder.

'I am talking about panacea; the one which cures all miseries of life.' he gave a smile.

'Ohhh..You are talking about that powder. I consumed it as Varun broke some bad news' I replied.

'Bad news.....I guess you and bad things have come connection.' He again gave a smile.

He was probably right.

'Actually we have spent all the money we had, even our credit cards will be blocked soon and we will be thrown out from the flat too.' I uttered all my miseries.

'You know I am lucky, one of my friends told me to use the credit card frequently. He knew that there would be a financial turbulence and no bank would get after you since they would be saving themselves from going bankrupt. I managed a platinum card from my dad, and believe me I used it like anything. I did all the shopping, got new music system, purchased antiques, whisky bottles and dined in five star hotels. And finally I threw away the card.' Abhi made me realize how unlucky I was; even I couldn't make use of the credit card.

Finally after driving for four hours we reached Kullu. The next task was to find her home. We started inquiring about her from many people. I had her snap in my mobile, many refused to identify her. We went to almost every shop and every beauty parlor but no one recognized her.

Finally one man recognized her.

'Ohhh...She was my neighbor.' I heaved a huge sigh of relief as the old man said that.

'So can you tell me where she resides?' Abhi asked the old man.

'Her house remains closed these days; I guess she has moved to some city. She had got a job in Surat but she left that job. Finally she is settled in Mumbai, her mom died last month and after that they have vacated this place; her retired father has gone with her. And they are living peacefully there.' The old man said and left.

Abhi looked towards me, 'You certainly have a bad luck; what's next now?'

'Let's go to her old house and I will inquire about her. We should find out where does she put up in Mumbai, it will be easy to trace her then' I thought it was the only option available.

'She is in Mumbai only, and we have come so far to search for her.' Abhi said.

Finally we reached her home. We inquired from her neighbors. They didn't have any clue as to where she lived in Mumbai.

'She has never contacted us after she left' one of them said.

'She must have got married by now' a few said.

No one had an exact knowledge of where she was living in Mumbai. Dejectedly we decided to return.

'Come on you should be happy; she is in Mumbai. You will find her there even if it's a big city. Don't be sad, she is so near to you and we came so far in search of her.' Abhi was becoming my good friend as he tried to lighten the moment.

We drove all the way back to Mumbai. None would believe that we had travelled 2000 kilometers on a bike. I went to Abhi's flat. We decided to booze for the last time, before we would part and get busy with our lives.

'What will you do after this? You won that reality show, so would you again try for Bollywood?' I asked the maverick Abhi.

He gave a big smile, 'I will enjoy my life and if I get time I would try for Bollywood.'

He was always relaxed or probably he never wanted to show his failures and dejection.

♥

I reached back to find Varun busy on my laptop.

'Hey, what happened? Did you meet Vidisha?' he gently asked.

'No. But she is in Mumbai.' I sat beside Varun.

'It's great news, you will find her soon.' Varun said.

'Probably...' I completed Varun's unspoken line.

'But the most important thing at this point of time is our meeting with the angel investor and we should focus on this. Vinod will join us tomorrow. So now please go through this plan and read this presentation before we finally present this to the investors.' Varun said and left the room.

I started going through the presentation made by Varun and Vinod.

As always I was again late in the morning, couldn't get up on time. Finally we flaunted our sophisticated dress and manners; were roaring to go to their office.

We reached the investors' office. The gate keeper escorted us to the waiting chamber. I was surprised to see Bankim Malpani as the head of that investing group. He was my team leader in the Money Bank.

'Hey Sir, how are you?' I said instantaneously on seeing my ex team leader.

'I am fine, Mr. Armaan. This world is indeed a circle. I never thought we would meet again' Mr. Malpani said as he took his seat.

'And we completed the circle, Sir' I replied.

'Don't call me Sir, Money Bank doesn't exist now.' He gave a smile.

I couldn't address him by his name since he was the only one who could have sponsored our start up and would take our life out of this dormant state.

Varun started the presentation and in no time he was over with the presentation. We handled all the questions intelligently and we were able to impress the Director of the investing group. After all, our idea was unique. We thought ahead of our competitors.

'There are so many online job portals in India. But your plan sounds unique; the features of your websites are also unique which will be an advantage to you. You will get more clients in a short span of time. But the idea is funny too.' Mr. Malpani said.

'Funny......In what sense?' Vinod asked.

'I mean your business plan sounds prominent, providing an online job portal service at the time of recession when most people are jobless and are getting thrown out from their jobs, is a smart move. Lots of people will hit your website. But the funny part is it will be started by a bunch of young people who themselves have lost them jobs.' Mr. Malpani exchanged a smile with me.

'But at least we thought of it and that is more important. Whatever was our past is indeed past, and no business is a hit at the time it starts. But we see a strong opportunity in this business. And I have always dreamt of being an entrepreneur.' Vinod made his point.

'Well said. But my advice to the young guns who want to own a firm is to keep calm and never be emotional while handling clients or your employees. Sentiments and business should never be mixed.

And you should always plan your business, keep an eye on your competitors and should strategize things intelligently. If you are not able to win by taking the right path, there is nothing wrong is taking wrong short cut methods. This is what my experience says. I was thrown out of my last job but still I managed a better paying job. But obviously you should not commit a crime; political moves, fake marketing stunts and inflating are permissible within a limit. The big MNCs do it and many others follow.' Malpani said.

'We will keep everything in our mind, after a brief discussion on our business plan'; Mr. Malpani decided to call off the meeting.

'You will get our mail on our stand of supporting your idea by tonight, so just wait for a few hours. And even if we are not able to support you, do take this plan to others. I guess you will definitely get some investors.' Mr. Malpani shook hands with every one of us.

Mr. Malpani asked me to stay while Vinod and Varun left. He took me out for coffee.

'Since I have worked with you, I know about your capability. You were promoted to the U.S in just three months which we couldn't do in fifteen years. But I never thought you would don an entrepreneur cap. I always thought that you wanted a high paying job. Isn't that true?' Mr. Malpani sipped his hot coffee.

'Frankly speaking whatever you said is true; I always wanted to have a high paying job. But I am supporting my friend's business because I want to start earning again and having one's own business is always the best thing' I sipped my coffee.

'Yeah, it's true. But an entrepreneur has a tough life, I don't know whether you can handle it or not because you were a trusting and an obedient employee who always want to have an easy life.' Mr.Malpani had a doubt about my intentions.

I never wanted to disclose that I was just doing it for the sake of our friendship. The business would obviously provide me with the money which I needed badly but after that I would definitely join some bank that pays highly. Till that time Vinod and Varun would have taken the company to new heights and they would have a good number of employees too. So they would never miss me.

'I believe this is the best I could do in my life. One's own company.' I stopped the insatiable debate.

'OK, then. I guess I can trust you all. Wait for a few hours before we make a final decision. A mail will reach you by tonight. And all the best for your future.' Mr. Malpani said and left.

I knew that he would definitely sponsor our start up; I could see the faith which he had in me and my friends. I had worked under him for two months and I could make out from his expression what he was thinking about.

'Few anxious hours, and then our lives will take a new path.' I thought, as I called Abhi to my flat for celebration.

Varun and Vinod were anxiously waiting for the mail.

'What do you think? Will they sponsor us?' Vinod asked me as I entered the room.

'Yeah.......' I gave a smile.

Finally there was a mail in Vinod's mailbox. We started praying. Vinod shouted; our eyes still closed with fear.

'Yes we made it!' Vinod said again.

I was hearing good news after so many days. Varun and Vinod's hard work clicked. Everyone got into celebration mode. Abhi soon joined it.

We decided to booze; took even the last penny we had. Everyone was ecstatic. Vinod clinked his glass with mine.

'Talent is definitely recession proof.' Varun said as he kept on drinking.

'One can definitely change his life whenever he wants. When the spirit is low and things are not going your way; the best thing is to be patient and keep moving. We won the battle because we dreamt and we really made an effort to fulfill it.' Vinod was the happiest person as he always wanted to be an entrepreneur.

'From tomorrow our lives will change. A new morning, a new life waits for us. Imagine our own office, we being the head, making this venture a successful one, earning hell of a lot of money and employing others. The time is not far when we will be business barons.' Varun was optimistic.

Everyone had a dream in their eyes and we knew the bad phase of our lives was over. Abhi was just silent and kept on enjoying the drink. We started talking of our office, the locality where we would take space for the office and all the minute details. We were behaving like a kid who came up with flying colors after failing many times. Our happiness knew no bounds.

'We have seen the struggle of life, the dark phase of life, got momentary success then lost the job but finally we managed to come out of the hangover of our past. But from now on we need to be more cautious and patient. Big things in life come with big responsibilities and one has to perform with excellence. So getting there was tough but the path would get tougher, so we have to perform all the time.' Vinod's words sounded sensible even when we were drunk.

'Don't worry, we will respond to the occasion intelligently.' I said.

'But I am sorry for whatever misunderstanding we had last time when we tried for investors. And I must thank Vinod for giving me a chance to be with you all.' I stopped.

'I always knew about your capability and intellectual power.' Vinod appreciated my qualities.

'Hey, why are you all getting emotional now? Just enjoy. Cheers.........' Abhi said loudly.

And our celebration continued till late into the night..........

When politics & youngism struck....

We started our business and opened our office in Andheri. We started doing publicity of our newly found company. We started getting some clients but we needed more clients. I was sitting with Abhi when suddenly my phone rang.

I went to the terrace; a light soothing breeze was blowing. I looked at the street which was jam-packed with traffic. The vehicles were honking and were waiting in the long queue.

'Please rush to Hiranandani Hospital, Varun had an accident' the female voice said. Suddenly one of the trucks blew the horn; the horn echoed in my ears.

'What??? Who is this?' I couldn't recognize the voice.

'Ananya' she said and rang off.

I couldn't understand what was going on, Varun was not in contact with Ananya; how come she called me. And what happened to Varun? Questions were popping up in my mind as I rushed to the hospital.

I checked at the hospital reception and ran towards Varun's room. Varun was seriously injured, and a girl was sitting near her. She was probably Ananya.

'What happened to him?' I asked Ananya without even introducing myself.

'He has been a victim of the anti-Bihari violence which is burning

Mumbai. There is a growing degree of xenophobia, racial discrimination, prejudice and violence in the city.' She said.

The article on Anti-Bihari attacks which I has seen in the newspaper last night appeared in my mind. It began when one of the top notch political leaders gave an open statement of racial discrimination against migrants from Bihar and U.P. He even accused these migrants of loitering around in the city and making it dirty. He accused these migrants of taking away jobs from the state people. He even called their auspicious festival, 'Chhat puja' as the cause of polluting the sea shores. There was a mass protest against it and at last the sufferers were the drivers of autorickshaws, taxis, vendors and the common man who belonged to North India. They were brutally beaten up and the movement was revolutionizing Mumbai. Many migrants returned to their state and many cities in Maharashtra were burning with racial discrimination. People were killing each other; there was complete disorder in the state.

'What the hell is this?' Abhi shouted.

I came to my senses on hearing Abhi's words.

'This is India, a true communist country' I went near Varun; he was still not in his senses. The marks of the cut were deep; he was still trembling with fear.

'Don't they understand? Aren't we human beings? We also live in India. There is nothing called my state and your state. But these are the people who drive the system and they themselves are behaving like criminals. Killing people, introducing racial discrimination amongst people.' Abhi understood the pain of being called a refugee in one's own country.

'Can't we do anything?' Ananya said.

'We are individuals, we can't do anything. If we raise our voice against them we will be killed. It's better to remain dormant for some time, things would automatically be normal. People will get used to their lives and then will forget everything until some other politician unearths such issues,' Abhi said as Varun started making some movement.

'Are you fine?' I instantaneously asked Varun on seeing his movements.

'I will be fine. Don't worry. There were thousands of people blocking the western highway; the rowdy crowds were abusing our state. They torched many buses and forcibly stopped the autos and other vehicles. After ascertaining the identity of the person; they started beating up if he was not from Maharashtra. I was travelling in a taxi and was on my way to Andheri, when these people caught my taxi; they burned it completely, bludgeoned the driver and started hitting me. Hundreds of people rushed towards me. They had weapons in their hand. No not hundred they were thousands....' Varun was terrified; his eyes looked scared and his body shook with fear.

'I was also passing through the western highway when I found a body lying on the road. The police was trying to control the mobs. And I never imagined we would meet again like this,' Ananya's voice broke. Varun held her hand demurely.

We were happy to see Varun back to his senses.

The tinsel town Mumbai kept on burning as the people from Bihar started vacating Maharashtra. The flight of business and capital increased unemployment, led to mass migration of Bihari farmers and unemployed youth to more developed states of India. Many saw Biharis, U.Pies as criminals and attribute any rise in criminality to Bihari youth, or the so called "Bihari Mafia". Due to the high levels of crime in Bihar there was a perception by some, that Biharis are inherently criminal by nature. This had led to Biharis being blamed for crimes ranging from automobile thefts to increase in rape, murder and kidnapping. One of the top notch leaders declared in the city that Biharis bring diseases, violence, job insecurity, and domination, wherever they go. The scenario became even worse. The leaders of the state started abusing each other. Some of the activists burnt effigies of these leaders without knowing what would be happening to a common man; they were forcibly inculcating hatred among different religions. The government at the centre couldn't do anything. There was protest in many parts of Bihar, but situation was getting out of control for Bombay police.

'What is happening to Bombay? Why is there so much hatred among people? Don't we belong to the same country?' I lighted my cigarette.

Varun was getting discharged and we were waiting for him outside the hospital.

'Bombay...'Abhi exclaimed.

'What happened?' I asked him.

'Don't even say it in front of the political group who are behind this atrocious act. They will think that you came here when this city was called Bombay and you never left it. It became your home.' Abhi lighted his cigarette.

'Yeah I know; our lives are at stake. And these politicians who hardly care for the people will decide our fate. Everything is a political stunt, just to win the general elections and have a monopoly. They can never allow any other political party to get settled in Mumbai' I took my seat in the taxi as Varun was brought outside.

Ananya was still with him, she loved him truly.

'So when are you getting married?' I asked Varun just to lighten the moment.

He gave a small smile and looked at Ananya like an obedient husband.

'Very soon', Ananya replied.

'Now that you are rich; you can marry her', Abhi giggled.

Varun and Ananya gave the maverick a tough look but he was hardly affected by those tough looks..

'Oh…it's great that you have decided to marry…'Abhi said and he ordered the driver of the taxi to take another route.

'Why are you taking this long route?' Varun asked.

'It's a safe route,' I said.

We were sitting in the front and the love birds were at the back of the taxi. Varun held Ananya's hand. A surprise was waiting for them.

'Thank you,' he said to her.

And they hugged each other.

'Hey...you can do all these things when you are alone.' Abhi winked at me.

Ananya was about to kiss Varun when Abhi interrupted again.

Suddenly Abhi ordered the driver to stop in front of a small temple.

'Let's go inside and take the blessings of God before we start our new life and new business,' Abhi said.

'And you the couple can have the blessings from God' I said as Abhi got busy on his phone.

We ordered Varun and Ananya to walk ahead of us. They climbed the staircase. The temple was decorated and there was a *pandit* sitting inside the temple.

Anaya held Varun's hand. They looked like a perfect couple.

'This looks like someone is getting married,' Ananya said to Varun.

'Yes. You and Varun are getting married today' I broke the surprising news.

'Yeah we have planned everything,' Abhi said.

The couple was surprised to hear it.

'What!!! Are you kidding?' Varun exclaimed.

'No it's wrong. My uncle and my brother should know about it.' Ananya said.

'Even they are here. Look inside the temple, they are sitting over there,' Abhi said.

He certainly had made all the preparations. I knew about his capability, he did everything with perfection.

He brought the bridal dress, bridegroom's gown, the flowers, the garlands, jewels and all the things required. There was a small room behind the temple, where Varun and Ananya changed their dresses. And the *pandit* started the marriage ceremony by chanting the holy *mantras*.

Abhi raised Varun on his shoulder while Ananya tried to put the garland around Varun. Finally I had to offer my shoulder to complete the ceremony. The couple laughed and finally tied the auspicious knot.

'Congratulations......' Abhi shouted.

I hugged Varun and Ananya. We escorted them to the car. Ananya was surprised to see the car as it was decorated with flowers and ribbons. Everything was happening too fast for them and they were unable to comprehend it.

Abhi opened the champagne bottle and splashed it around us. Varun was ecstatic. He was very happy and held Ananya's hand while she kept on blushing.

'Thank you so much.' Varun looked into my eyes.

'Friendship is the best thing one can have in life', Varun said and hugged Abhi.

'You owe us a party for this', Abhi said.

'Definitely.......' Ananya said as the couple went away.

We kept a few cards and gifts inside the car. Varun waved from the car.

'JUST MARRIED........' I read the message written on the back of the car and hugged Abhi for his help and generosity. We were definitely becoming lifetime friends.

'This was the only way to bring Varun out of the shock. I could see the fear in his eyes after being beaten up brutally. This was the only possible way to bring him back to his senses.' Abhi said, as we proceeded towards his bike.

'I know, whatever happened with him was injustice. I don't know how one feels when he is called a 'REFUGEE', 'A TRAITOR' in his own country. He has undergone that pain,' I followed Abhi.

'I would just hit the person, who calls me that,' Abhi lighted a cigarette and boasted of his muscular power.

'But can you do anything when a politician of a state calls you by that name and he even drags you outside the state by force?' I asked.

Abhi remained quiet.

'Do you have any answer?' I looked at Abhi who seemed as helpless as the people who were pushed out of the city and were referred to as a malady.

'But someone has to raise his voice; someone has to stand against this evil. India is still not independent; the great freedom fighters would be dejected if they had seen the current scenario of our nation. They wanted to build a nation for the people but these politicians, criminals and terrorists are messing up everything. I always thought that India was my homeland; I can roam in any place, work in any state, mix with and adapt to that culture.' Abhi was infuriated.

I hugged Abhi.

'A youth can change this society, this society is corrupt, the politics stinks and people behind such acts are not human beings. Even people of Mumbai know that whatever is going on is totally atrocious, illegal and bad. But no one will raise his voice. We are considered as common youth, living a common life and destined to die like a common man. Is it not our duty to attend the nation's call and do something for the nation rather than filling our pockets with green notes?' I asked Abhi who looked clueless for a moment.

'You are right dude; but what about the hot babes who are dying to sleep with us, what about our junk habits, no drugs, no intoxicating liquids, no money, no bikes and no enjoyment?' Abhi said looking into my eyes and suddenly lightened the moment.

'Everyday will be a dry day.........' I said to him with a smile on my face.

'Naaah..' I made my face.

'It's a bad idea to be in politics or being a rebel. We are happy with our usual lives. We are a new generation; Y generation youth' Abhi winked.

'Look at that babe; her beautiful face, her attractive body.' I pointed towards the girl walking on the road.

We were just like the youth who didn't do anything for the nation but would always demand rights from the government and point towards issues.

'Who will put their clean hands in the dirty world of politics and get their hands dirty when nothing is going to change?'

This was the motto of many youths across the country.

Mumbai was still burning with issues of racial discrimination. Violence continued for many days. People from north India and Bihar were tagged 'BIHARIS','BHAIYA'. The title was used openly in train, buses, roads and many suburbs.

We were still to recover from the shock of recession when foul politics struck. We wanted to do our business and contribute to society by offering jobs to many people, irrespective of their religion and their domicile state. But things weren't shaping up to our expectations.

One of the local advertising companies of Mumbai called us; they wanted to merge with us; they saw a potential growth in their profit after joining hands with us as they saw our company moving and capturing the market quite quickly. We created an opportunity when market had nothing to offer us.

Abhi and I took a taxi to the office of the advertising company. There was a lot of jam on the road which was a very common thing in Mumbai. We decided to walk to the office after waiting for thirty minutes. We came out and started walking with others. After walking a mile we boarded a BEST bus at Sakinaka and decided to use the local train from Kurla.

The double decker bus was moving swiftly. The bus was empty to our surprise, which was usually jam-packed during the rush hours. I looked outside the window; the soothing air hit my face. I looked keenly on the road as if my eyes were searching for Vidisha.

'I know we will meet one day; you are somewhere here only. I can feel you; Vidisha.' I said to myself when suddenly there was panic in the bus.

'No one should move, be seated,' a young man said with a country made revolver in his hand.

It was a bus hijack.

A twenty five year old man wielding a country made revolver, had taken control of the bus and had injured one passenger. His demands were unique. He was protesting against the attacks on north Indian who were candidates appearing for a railway examination recently. He wanted to talk to the Mumbai Police Commissioner and the media.

The bus stopped near Bail Bazaar police chowky in Kurla. The conductor alerted the cops. An angry young man brandished the revolver.

'I am not going to kill anyone; I am fighting for my rights, my state and my people,' The young man shouted at us.

We crouched in a corner of the bus, made no movement and looked at the rebellious man.

His eyes were burning with revenge.

Police surrounded the bus and approached the young man, but were fired at. They escaped unhurt and calls in forces. Hundred cops cordoned off the bus and asked four passengers to come down.

'Surrender yourself.......'the police officials spoke through loud speakers.

He wrote something on the currency note and threw the note

outside the bus towards the cops; we didn't make any noise. The angry man brandished the revolver, asked to speak to the media and the police chief. Police again asked him to surrender, but he threw down currency notes claiming he had come to kill the politician.

'I am not going to kill any innocent people, I always knew what loss is, and I just want that bloody politician who calls me a refugee in my own country, in front of me. I want to kill him. I came here to study; I came here to establish my career. I am just like you, a common youth wanting to clean his house, his country.' The young guy said with a red eye.

On seeing the police approaching the bus he fired in the air. Police retaliated. He fired a bullet at a policeman. He shot four bullets from an illegal country-made revolver, one at a policeman trying to reach the bus's upper deck, one into the thigh of a passenger and a couple in the air. The bullet kissed Abhi's thigh and blood came gushing out. All of us in the bus were terrified.

A special team of officers entered the bus and went to the upper deck of the bus. Three police officers fired thirteen shots, four of which hit this man. Three hit him in the head and one went through his heart.

The young guy fell to his knees and finally died. He was definitely neither a criminal nor a terrorist; he was just a common man like us. Death is something which brings tears even to the eyes of a cruel man but he didn't have any fear; he was on his own mission; a mission that was never achieved. He was lying dead in front of us.

Police surrounded the bus; we rushed out of the bus. We couldn't believe our eyes; a youth died in an encounter in front of our eyes. He was certainly not a criminal but he was treated like a criminal.

I took Abhi to the hospital.

All the newspapers made that young guy named Pranaw as their hero. He was just twenty five years old and belonged to Patna. Media raised questions about the police officials for killing the young guy as he was not a criminal. Many projected him as the youth of today's generation who take hasty decision and want to change the society.

'I want to talk to the police commissioner; call the media. I don't want to kill anyone; I just want to kill the politician behind this discrimination.' Pranaw wrote this on a currency note and threw it to the police. This goes to show that the encounter was a wrong step; reported one of the newspapers.

I was reminded of the scene when Pranaw wrote that on the currency note.

'Pranaw was not a criminal. His intention was to draw public and government attention to the tirade started by the activists against north Indians. He had no past criminal record and so one cannot compare his case with other encounters in which hardened criminals are killed by the police.' Abhi said.

'According to the Code of Conduct for Law Enforcement Officials adopted by UN General Assembly resolution 34/169 of 17 December 1979, Article 3 states that, "Law enforcement officials may use force only when strictly necessary and to the extent required for the performance of their duty." I said as I knew some nuances of law.

'Yes that's true; he didn't have any criminal background so the police personnel should have tried to arrest him rather than engaging him in an encounter'. Abhi replied.

He gave his life just to prove that whatever was going on was indeed an atrocious act. Such people will be born again whenever there is a crime, in society.

'It was not a criminal who died, it was not a son who died, it was not a brother who died, it was not a martyr who died, but he was a youth who died. He was the future of the country; a youth lost in this way is certainly a loss to the country.' Abhi was touched by the entire event.

'One youth lost is not one youth less; its one more youth born out of those circumstances.' I wrote a blog on it.

'I am going to stand against the evils in the country; I won't mind giving up my life but I won't bear this. I am not a REFUGEE in this country.' Abhi said as he was angry with the entire system.

'I also want the same, this is my country. I should go to any state; roam anywhere in India and no one should point to me or raise the issue of my regionalism and my domicile state.' I replied.

'Society is corrupt; many leaders are corrupt. The powers are vested in such corrupt hands; how can you expect the country to grow? I am the youth; I am supposed to be the fate of this country, if I don't care for my motherland; who will care for it? I am joining politics. I want to change the society; the system controlling us' Abhi declared.

'Are you nuts? Don't take such hasty decisions in life. I know you are angry but there are many other ways to be heard. Politics is not an easy thing.' I tried to lesser Abhi's frustration.

'I am gonna change. Now I am cleaning up and I am moving on. Going straight and choosing life. No drugs, no syringes and no fun. I am looking for it already. I am gonna be just like you; a normal human being. I will quit everything and will be a good citizen. I will definitely join politics. My soul can hear the call from my nation. My nation needs my services. I guess this is the only thing I could do in my life. I am definitely not doing social service; I am doing everything for myself and for my satisfaction.' Abhi said.

Giving life for the nation was stuffy text book material, for us but many freedom fighters gave it and we don't know whether the death of this youth was equal to that them. His approach might be wrong for many but was there an alternative to stop the killings of the innocent people? We never thought that we would start discarding our own homemade theories.

One night Abhi came frantically searching for me.

'Common man, wake up. The city is burning; I have brought something for you.' He shouted.

He took me outside.

I was totally clueless of what was going on.

He took me to the society's gymnasium. We sat on the bench placed in front of the red wall.

'Hey, I have brought something for you' Abhi said lighting his cigarette.

I looked with curiosity towards Abhi.

Abhi took out a whisky bottle and made two pegs.

'What!!! We came here to drink; we could have done this in room.' I said out of anger.

'First drink this; I have a gift for you.' Abhi passed the disposable glass to me.

After gulping two pegs; he unfolded a paper.

'This is your gift' He handed the gift folded in paper to me.

'A country made revolver' I shouted and was shocked.

'Yes; it's meant for your protection.' Abhi sounded like a drunkard.

'Are you mad? This is dangerous and insane.' I handed over the pistol back to Abhi.

'And whatever is happen... killing people; fucking all the city is not a crime; the... consequences so why should we.' They don't worry about t... demands were unique.

'Remember whatever happened with... can happen with you; you might not be lucky all the time. Just ... this with you; it will help you in those circumstances.' Abhi force... revolver back in my hand.

We gulped the last peg and Abhi left.

I was sitting alone holding the revolver. 'Is this the only solution?' I thought. I saw the newspaper lying by my side which mentioned about the collapse of the Wall Street. I got illusions of my past and then I dozed off.

Days passed away; everything took a political turn; all the political parties jumped in, ministers, M.Ps, MLAs everyone came out and gave their views on it. But no one gave a guarantee that such rave...ous act would never be repeated.

Days passed; people got accustomed to their lives and forgot the past. Varun returned from his week long break after celebrating his honey moon in Goa. Violence stopped in Maharashtra as the police and the government came down hard on the activists.

Vinod was still working hard for the start up. Varun joined him. In less than a year the company flourished and we were millionaires. We created everything starting from scratch. We had no option; the market was slow, there was hardly any job for us. We created opportunities for ourselves.

I was still occupied with the thoughts of Vidisha; I searched for

…er frantically in the city w… …nding her.

Our company got se… one of the best start ups opened in India, our fate change… …nly. Our company reached new heights. Varun decided to th… big party for our success, he also announced the opening of … corporate office in Mumbai which would provide emplo… …nt to hundred people and would give jobs in time of recession.

Many m…nisters, politicians and the media were invited to the award ceremony. Abhi had already planned the evening. We would go for a big treat after the felicitation of our start up. Everyone was ecstatic but I felt lost.

It was the biggest business awarding group; the Chief Minister of the state was the chief guest. We reached the five star hotel where the award ceremony was planned.

'Varun, I am sorry but I have thought a lot on this. I am not an entrepreneur like you; I am more suitable for a job rather than being an owner. I guess you would understand my decision of quitting the position of director. I want to search my love; my life is empty without her. Please let me go, our friendship will always remain alive. I hope you will respect my personal decision.' I donned the courage to blurt out everything which was cooking in my mind. I was feeling like this after meeting Mr. Malpani but I wanted to help my friends.

'I respect your decision. This company will always be open for you, whenever you want to work with us, do join us. You are one of the best professionals I have come across in my life. But you have to join the party this evening', Varun exchanged a smile.

'I would definitely join it. We worked really hard for it,' I said to Varun and left the office.

Vinod was busy with the arrangements for the gathering in the night. He had hired a few security personnel to ensure the smooth functioning of the meeting and the bash.

Few ministers and M.Ps joined us. The corporate office was inaugurated by them and there was a big celebration. Vinod had booked the hall inside a multi storied 5 star hotel for our own bash after the award ceremony.

Finally we were declared as the best start up in the country by an agency and NEN start up. Vinod and Varun went on the dais to receive the trophy.

We all went on the dais to receive our coveted win, the trophy. The mike was handed over to us to give a short speech on our success.

"All the big companies were once a start up and all the start ups were once an idea." Vinod started.

'Huh…An IDEA indeed. An idea is the one that can change the course of the world. An idea is like the rays of the sun cutting through the darkness of life and illuminating the path. An idea is nothing but a dead matter; you have to water it and make it lively by making efforts. We knew this business would definitely click as the moment demanded it. It sounds humorous, isn't it? Providing jobs in recession but an entrepreneur is born when he sees an opportunity, an opportunity to change his life and that of others. Most of the entrepreneurs are the ones who have been unsuccessful in life and in their careers. They start their business just to have a continuous source of income; few of my team members are like that but I always had a vision that this was going to click. I would be more ecstatic when I see JOBS MADE EASY as one of India's biggest placement consultancy. This is just a start. Sky is not the limit for us; we want to enter in all the planets.' Vinod's speech was applauded by many.

Vinod passed the mike to Varun.

'I AM BROKE... LOVE ME. You say that I belong to a different state but I belong to the same country. You called me a disease. Yes; I have a disease............A disease to work hard and to do my job honestly. You have beaten me up and others because I am not from your state. But this state is no different from mine, people here drink water, eat food, they are fed by the same air, atmosphere, sun, moon, food, clothes etc. They laugh, they cry; everything is the same throughout the country; then why is there so much hatred among different communities? You say we bring violence and job insecurity to different states but we are the ones who are the part of your daily life, many from that part of India come here; they take a job of driving taxis, rickshaws, auto rickshaws, they work in factories as labor, they are building construction labors, railway staff, IAS officers, politicians, industrialists, bureaucrats. We do all kinds of things just to earn some money; if you politicians care for the common people just do something to remove unemployment, every other thing and crime will stop eventually. I am not a politician but I know it's wrong to introduce discrimination and it's not acceptable. You can't stop unemployment by deporting people; you are ministers, government; you can open up new sectors and new windows for unemployed people. Nobody is forcibly taking someone's job. I am dejected and I am certainly broke when I see my country lagging behind others and fighting on such issues.' Varun blurted out whatever he felt; he was the one who had received slaps and punches for being a refugee. He bravely looked towards the politicians.

He looked dejected and started again "All times are beautiful for those who maintain joy within them; but there is no happy or favorable time for those with disconsolate souls. Today things have changed quite dramatically. Optimism has replaced pessimism in every youngster's mind. Everyone is out in the sun trying to change things for them. I was just another common person like you, trying to manage a job in such turbulent times but was rejected wherever I went. But I never lost hope; I kept fighting and trying. But the best thing which I could have done was to move on in life. I never looked back and had any regret because I always knew that my talent and my potentials would always remain with me. And then we dreamt of this company and we made it possible. Believe me, 'TALENT IS CERTAINLY RECESSION PROOF'. If you are true to your work; you will definitely manage a job. Time was tough; we didn't see much opportunity in the market, instead we created an opportunity. We could have easily given up our lives like many did after losing a job but we maintained joy in ourselves and our zeal to excel increased. We got hungrier and worked even harder. This is just a beginning; bring whatever obstacles you can bring in my path; just bring it, lay a mountain in front of us. I will laugh at it; our exuberance, youthful nature and dedication will surmount everything. This is because I am a YOUTH and my reach, energy and enthusiasm to excel is endless. I am a YOUTH.' Varun gave a mind blowing speech.

'Life is all about playing gamble and taking risks; you have to take your chances. We took it when no one was offering any job to us and believe me we will be at a better position than many of those who said to us that you are immature youth. This evening was possible because of our efforts. We always stood as a team and we will definitely be the best job portal service in India' Varun stopped and held Vinod's hand. Confidence was reflecting on the two youths.

Finally it was my turn to speak some golden words and praise our effort and our company. I was high with four pegs which I took with Abhi while coming.

"I am just another common youth who sometimes gets caught in rain, sometimes in blasts, and sometimes in anti-Bihari protest. I am the one who suffers the most be it a traffic jam, protests, elections, racial discrimination and curfews. I have been called immature, tagged as a maverick but I am a youth whose potentials are great. I came here with a hell of a lot of failures; I came here for tasting sweet success. Coming up here I have no hidden agenda, I will speak what I felt and what I saw. Losing my future is not losing an election or losing some points on the stock exchange. I am here to speak for countless people who dream and have faced recession. I was thrown out of my job in the U.S. I came back to India, dejected. The world came crashing down, but still I maintained the joy within myself and kept on trying for new jobs. Time was tough, nothing was going my way but I never lost hope. I entered the world of drugs but I came out of it too. I would have easily given up my life like many did but I was not ready to surrender myself as I wanted to fight. And believe me this was the best thing anyone can do, we kept on struggling and finally we created an opportunity for us when the market didn't provide any opportunity." I gave a short pause and exchanged a smile with Vinod.

"I am a YOUTH, I can do anything and my reach is endless. I have been tagged for doing nothing and just enjoying my life, smoking, drinking and consuming drugs but we are the future of this nation. Look around the world and see the problems, the foul politics where ministers make money and then another comes just to spoil the society. Who cares for the nation? I saw my career lying in a gutter; I faced the recession, lost my love and was beaten up in my own country. I am dejected. I AM BROKE, LOVE ME…!I am Broken; Love me because I am like you all, I am just another human being trying to earn money and do my job. There is nothing like my state and your state, there is only one thing- our country which we have to make better. There are some politicians who are loyal and are running this country but most of them are corrupt. I would like to ask you all a very simple question" I looked at my audience which consisted of politicians, general crowd and representatives of some more companies. But I knew whatever I would say would be telecast since there was a long queue of media and newspaper reporters.

"How many of you actually go out on Independence Day to salute our national flag? How many sing the national anthem on Republic Day? Most of us take these days as national holidays and we enjoy the holidays by either sleeping or by remaining at home with our families. Isn't it correct?" A long buzz ran around.

"We expect so much from our country; but we hardly do anything for it. But our main problem is, instead of fighting the situation and system we get complacent and get use to our lives, situation and forgets everything going around. This is our main problem, we forget everything. I belong to north India; I would not disclose the name of my domicile state, I will be attacked if I disclose; it maybe my offices will be burnt but I don't fear now. I will raise my voice. We are the ones, who saw the bloody discrimination; who became a victim of such protests. I know what it feels like when you are called a REFUGEE in your own country. I am certainly not a refugee, this country is mine and I can go anywhere I want. But the politics stinks, they are criminals moving openly. If people are migrating then why these ministers don't create opportunities for them in their state, they just talk and give big lectures. This is not acceptable, this system is fraud." I hit the podium with my right hand.

"The demand of the hour is YOUTH. We will join politics, will become bureaucrats. India will change. I heard the call from my nation; I heard it late but I am happy at least I heard it. We will open our up companies, we will be the entrepreneurs of tomorrow and we can definitely change the nation. Did you have to worry about these things when you were young? I too don't have a solution but I want to fight. The good I do, people will forget overnight. I will do good anyways coz finally it's between me and my nation; it was never between them anyways." I stopped as the hall went silent, politicians could see my eyes and suddenly everyone started clapping.

'Who are you? Is Pranaw your relative or you are awake because a youth died in front of you?' a media spokesman raised his issues.

'I am a youth who wants to make his country clean; the country that has been polluted with foul politics and corruption. And Pranaw was not my relative but should I wait for that time when any of my relative gets killed in such incidents? And why are you having problems if I feel awakened? I was always dissatisfied by the system going around, but I couldn't get time as I was running after money. But now I am free and will stand up for my nation.' I answered.

The media kept on aggravating my grief.

'Abhi; just shut the door' I messaged Abhi; when suddenly the main gate was closed.

The security personnel of the C.M surrounded him and positioned themselves.

'I took my revolver out.' There was a complete panic in the hall.

'Don't worry; I won't kill anyone. I could have killed a few bastards behind this atrocious act; but I love humanity and I don't want to destroy it. I placed the gun near my head. Is this what you all want? You want to throw me out of this state; you want to raise questions. It's no use killing you all; better I die rather than facing such things. But please help me; my nation; cure the disease which is gripping my nation' I addressed to the C.M.

"I am broke. Love me..! Accept me," I addressed the speech to the politicians, ministers and all those whose minds have become dirty due to racial discrimination. The security personnel surrounded me and forcibly took the revolver.

'Why don't you join politics?' few politicians asked me.

'I am happy; I don't want to be corrupt; I will work independently' I said to them.

The police arrested me. After holding up for few hours; the security personnel after inquiring my identity left me and escorted me to the gate as I was just a mango man (*aam aadmi*).

I left the place and came out in the open. A ring ceremony was going on in the banquet hall of the hotel on the ground floor. She was the same girl whom I had seen.

Some 30 minutes before:

"A girl wearing a pink sari passed me; I turned back to have a look at her. She was probably getting married. Her movements and the style of walking seemed unique. Her fragrance seemed familiar. I looked at her but couldn't see her face as she kept on walking. I was getting late for the award ceremony; I rushed towards the hall through the main gate" It was just thirty minutes before.

I came outside the hall; the gathering in the banquet hall attracted me. I lighted my cigarette and went near them. I saw that woman wearing a pink sari but still couldn't see her face. The ring ceremony was going on; I thought of congratulating the couple, and went near them.

Suddenly I felt Vidisha's presence around me; I looked here and there. Finally I reached near the couple by pushing the crowd, surrounding the couple.

The woman looked at me. I was stunned, my roving eyes made no movement and my breath stopped.

'Vidisha........'I said.

Her appearance hadn't changed. I was seeing her after a year; she still looked elegant and beautiful. Her smile would still make a drooping flower bloom; her fragrance was still there in my breath. Her beautiful face would make anyone forget his problems and would soothe the dejected heart.

'Armaan.......'she said.

I didn't understand what to do or to curse myself. I knew my bad luck would never leave me. I hesitantly approached them; presented a fake smile and congratulated them. Vidisha's eyes were fixed on me.

"I wish you have a happy married life....' Finally I shook hands with Vidisha and turned away. Vidisha wanted to say something but it was too late now.

Tears started rolling down my cheeks. I had lost my love.

I went to the open terrace; it was deserted. I stood on the terrace and kept on looking at the busy road when suddenly someone touched my shoulder. I turned to have a look, it was Vidisha.

'I am sorry...'Vidisha said.

'It's OK, it's my bad luck. I went to your home town in search of you and came to know from there that you were in Mumbai. I never thought we would meet this way. But I missed you a lot. I always saw you in my dreams, you instilled self confidence in me, I would have given up my life but it was you and your thoughts which kept me sane and breathing. I can never forget you; I don't know how I would manage without you. I will always love you........' I couldn't stop expressing my feelings, and my tears.

'I wanted to tell you about my marriage and I tried too, but I couldn't find you. My father wanted to marry me off.....'Vidisha said.

'You are still very beautiful. Don't look at me this way, I will again fall for you.' I held Vidisha's hand.

'My love didn't win but it will be always with me making me happy and sad sometimes. I will cherish the moments spent with you. Our love will live in this world even after our death. I don't know how I will manage without you. I will always love you...........'my voice broke as I kissed that beautiful hand.

Tears came rolling down her cheeks, I wiped her tears.

'Please don't cry; it's your special day. I don't want tears in your eyes because of me; your make up will also wash away and then no one will recognize you.' I tried to laugh hiding my tears.

She gave a small smile.

'I am sorry. I will always love you too..............' She kissed me on my cheeks.

I held her shoulders and she gave a sweet kiss on my lips.

It was probably 'A LAST KISS.' A kiss that made me fall in love all over again. She took a few steps backwards, suddenly turned away and left. I stood there and tears wouldn't stop rolling down.

♥

A week passed. JOBS MADE EASY was going strong in the market. I resigned from the post of director.

'I am getting married; my father wants to marry me off. Please come and take me away. We will run away and will create a new world of happiness. We will have a family, our children and we would live together till we die.......' I read Vidisha's mail. She had written it a few days back, I cursed myself for not checking my mails. I closed the mail box, but couldn't control my emotions.

The stock market started rising again; few companies started hiring again. The financial meltdown was finally over and the market was behaving normally. Many jobless youths got jobs.

Soon Abhi contested for the post of an M.P and got a seat. I too joined that political party and thought of implementing changes in the society. We started our own small political party YLP (youth liberation party) that was more of a rebellious group and we worked for the upliftment of the society, addressed issues of racial discrimination; poverty and employment pressurized the government to take necessary action. Many youth joined us. We never cared for our lives; protested in front of Prime Minister's house when occasion demanded. We realized the true potential of youth. We were beaten up many a times by the police while protesting; but it didn't have any impact on us.

I was taking a stroll on my terrace when someone knocked on my door. I was surprised to see Vidisha again.

'If we run away from our home today, I will do any job. I will always love you and we will get married. If our family accepts us then we will come back otherwise we will make our own small world full of love. What do you say? Let's run away, the setting is perfect for it.' She blinked her eyes and made me remember my dialogue which I had said when I met her on the train.

She gave a card; hesitantly I opened it.

'What...!!!' I exclaimed. It was like a puzzle for me.

It was the same card which I had gifted her on the farewell. The card was a collage of Vidisha's snap and at the bottom it was written by me, 'You are the only person who can make my life beautiful as these flowers and beautiful pictures. I am leaving a small black and white sketch of mine; fill in the colors and make my life colorful and beautiful.

'You idiot, try to help me and bring my luggage inside. I did not marry him, after you left. I told everything to my father and the guy to whom I was going to get married. My marriage was called off. Look at your room, it's so dirty.' She looked very normal and exchanged a big smile; started arranging stuff kept on the shelf; kept the linens in the washing machine.

She had filled colors in my sketch; she colored it with red and pink.

'I colored it red as light red represents joy, sexuality, passion, sensitivity, and love. I want you to love me with passion. Pink signifies romance, love, and friendship. We will always be best friends even after marriage; our love and romance will never die. You had me at the farewell day. I really thought about you when you were not in front of me; your thought brought smile on my face. I need you by my side to share and care. You are my desire, my happiness, and my dream; let us live happily today, tomorrow and forever' I read the card.

'Nothing gonna change my love for you; I will love you till I die and even beyond that. You are my sunshine, my angel, be mine forever.' I hugged her; held her hand and went on my knees; she presented her beautiful hand; we danced.

I shut the main door of my room... She started kissing me and we made love......